SHIPMENT 1

Paging Dr. Right by Stella Bagwell
Her Best Man by Crystal Green
I Do! I Do! by Pamela Toth
A Family for the Holidays by Victoria Pade
A Cowboy Under Her Tree by Allison Leigh
Stranded with the Groom by Christine Rimmer

SHIPMENT 2

All He Ever Wanted by Allison Leigh
Prescription: Love by Pamela Toth
Their Unexpected Family by Judy Duarte
Cabin Fever by Karen Rose Smith
Million-Dollar Makeover by Cheryl St.John
McFarlane's Perfect Bride by Christine Rimmer

SHIPMENT 3

Taming the Montana Millionaire by Teresa Southwick
From Doctor...to Daddy by Karen Rose Smith
When the Cowboy Said "I Do" by Crystal Green
Thunder Canyon Homecoming by Brenda Harlen
A Thunder Canyon Christmas by RaeAnne Thayne
Resisting Mr. Tall, Dark & Texan by Christine Rimmer
The Baby Wore a Badge by Marie Ferrarella

SHIPMENT 4

His Country Cinderella by Karen Rose Smith
The Hard-to-Get Cowboy by Crystal Green
A Maverick for Christmas by Leanne Banks
Her Montana Christmas Groom by Teresa Southwick
The Bounty Hunter by Cheryl St.John
The Guardian by Elizabeth Lane

SHIPMENT 5

Big Sky Rancher by Carolyn Davidson
The Tracker by Mary Burton
A Convenient Wife by Carolyn Davidson
Whitefeather's Woman by Deborah Hale
Moon Over Montana by Jackie Merritt
Marry Me...Again by Cheryl St.John

SHIPMENT 6

Big Sky Baby by Judy Duarte
The Rancher's Daughter by Jodi O'Donnell
Her Montana Millionaire by Crystal Green
Sweet Talk by Jackie Merritt
Big Sky Cowboy by Jennifer Mikels
Montana Lawman by Allison Leigh
Montana Mavericks Weddings
by Diana Palmer, Susan Mallery

SHIPMENT 7

You Belong to Me by Jennifer Greene
The Marriage Bargain by Victoria Pade
It Happened One Wedding Night by Karen Rose Smith
The Birth Mother by Pamela Toth
A Montana Mavericks Christmas
by Susan Mallery, Karen Rose Smith
Christmas in Whitehorn by Susan Mallery

SHIPMENT 8

In Love with Her Boss by Christie Ridgway
Marked for Marriage by Jackie Merritt
Rich, Rugged...Ruthless by Jennifer Mikels
The Magnificent Seven by Cheryl St.John
Outlaw Marriage by Laurie Paige
Nighthawk's Child by Linda Turner

HER
BEST MAN

CRYSTAL GREEN

HARLEQUIN® MONTANA MAVERICKS

Special thanks and acknowledgment are given
to Crystal Green for her contribution to the
MONTANA MAVERICKS: STRIKING IT RICH miniseries.

ISBN-13: 978-0-373-41803-9

Recycling programs
for this product may
not exist in your area.

Her Best Man

Printed in U.S.A.

www.Harlequin.com

Crystal Green lives near Las Vegas, where she writes for the Harlequin Special Edition and Harlequin Blaze lines. She loves to read, overanalyze movies and TV programs, practice yoga, and travel when she can. You can read more about her at crystal-green.com, where she has a blog and contests. Also, you can follow her on Twitter, @CrystalGreenMe.

To Beverly, whose art is eternal, too.

Chapter One

One would think Allaire Traub would be smart enough to recognize her best friend across a parking lot. But when she first saw him, she had no idea it was the man she used to call "her D.J."

Tori Jones, Allaire's friend and fellow teacher, spotted him first as they walked into the parking lot of Thunder Canyon High School. Both her and Allaire's arms were loaded with lesson plans and workbooks, their cheeks already reddened by a cool September wind.

"Please tell me that's one of my students' parents just dropping in for a conference," Tori said.

Trying to get a bead on who her friend was referring to, Allaire whisked a strand of blond hair out of her eyes. Across the lot, the school band practiced their competition show. A coach's whistle trilled from the football field to the east.

Her gaze soon fell on a man standing with his back to them, hands in his jeans pockets while he watched the band easing into formation. His shoulders were broad beneath his suede-and-sheepskin coat, his dark brown hair tufted by the same breeze that was presently sending a shiver over Allaire herself.

Without quite knowing what she was doing, she ran her eyes over his body. Nice. Jeans molded over well-muscled legs. His stance was casual, confident. Her art teacher's fingers itched to shape him, to sculpt and feel.

But…nope, not for her, even if she did like what she saw. These days, Allaire didn't have the will to invest herself in dating, much less the emotion it took to be intimate with someone. Divorce had sapped the energy right out of her and, even if her marriage had dissolved four years ago, it didn't feel like enough time had passed to "get out there" again.

However, four years *was* enough time to get

into the habit of being a single woman who depended only on herself, and Allaire had discovered she hadn't minded that so much.

Really.

She shot Tori an encouraging grin. "You'd better hope he's not the parent of a failing student. That'd be fun."

The strawberry-blonde shrugged goodnaturedly, wrinkling her nose as she smiled, too. A light spray of freckles added a pixie-like vibe to Tori's short, wispy haircut. She was so hip that you could tell she'd moved here from a big city like Denver.

"Please," Tori said. "I don't mix business with pleasure. Look but don't touch. That's what I say—unless the looking comes during my off hours."

"More power to you then…." Allaire trailed off as the man across the parking lot turned around.

It was as if he'd been tuned in to her presence, sensing the moment she'd walked out of the school. Then again, it'd always been that way with the two of them.

A couple of peas in a pod, Allaire thought, as the man in the sheepskin coat smiled at her.

"D.J.?" she whispered.

He sauntered toward them while the band started to play, horns blaring and echoing through a big blue sky already painted with strokes of pinkened clouds.

"Who's D.J.?" Tori asked.

Good question, Allaire thought. Who *was* Dalton James Traub nowadays? She'd thought she'd known the answer all those years ago, when they'd been best friends throughout school.

When he'd been the best man at her wedding to his older brother, Dax.

Allaire paused, then smiled, the gesture weighing on her lips. "D.J.'s a…pal. Someone I haven't seen in a long, long time."

"Then I'll leave you to him," Tori said. "I need to get home and grade a batch of essays about *Moby Dick,* anyway. And, truly, I just can't wait to read all the veiled phallic jokes in store for me. Wish me patience and good humor?"

All Allaire could do was nod as her friend headed toward her compact car. The wind flirted with Tori's oversized coat and jaunty red scarf as she left Allaire to fend for herself.

Not only had she not *seen* D.J. in years, she hadn't talked to him in a long, long time, either. They'd started floating apart ten years ago after graduation, when he'd gone across the country for college. She'd seen him at her wedding, of course, but things had been too crazy for them to really enjoy each other's company. Then he'd left Thunder Canyon for good, except for a quick trip to his dad's funeral five years ago, just before she and Dax had divorced. Even then, she and her old friend hadn't talked to any extent—she'd just seen D.J. at the service, and he'd disappeared immediately afterward.

Stung, she'd been reluctant to call or e-mail, thinking he was avoiding her for a reason, probably because of her strained marriage to his brother. She'd even believed that D.J. might be taking Dax's side, even if they weren't the closest of brothers. She didn't know why that was—neither D.J. nor Dax ever wanted to talk about it. Still, blood was thicker than water, so she hadn't chanced the contact with D.J., afraid of how much an official rejection from him would hurt.

Now, as he approached, his gait slowed. He actually seemed more self-aware with each closing step.

Would he be uncomfortable around her now

that she and Dax were kaput? And what would she and D.J. have to say to each other after all these years?

As he got closer, Allaire's pulse picked up speed. It was a new feeling, at least around good ol' D.J., and she didn't understand why a mere glimpse of him across the parking lot had changed things.

Allaire searched for reasons: her heart was bippity-bopping because she was nervous about seeing him again, that's all. She wasn't a big social type, anyway, not unless you counted her new friendship with Tori. Marriage to Dax had been her world until it'd collapsed; she'd married young and never thought to make any friends because she'd had him.

Besides, D.J. was Dax's brother. Her *ex*'s brother. There was no place for accelerated pulses here.

D.J. stopped a proper distance away, but it was close enough for her to see how brown his eyes still were, how his cheeks still got those ruddy stains in cold weather, how his hair still refused to keep to its combed style.

Yet there was something different about him now—*a lot* different. He'd grown up, his face leaner, more angled—sloped cheekbones, a firm chin with a slight dimple.

Allaire's heart tilted, as if reconsidering him.

"I thought that was you," he said, voice much lower, manlier, than the D.J. she remembered. Had he sounded like this when they'd fleetingly greeted each other at the funeral?

His tone sent a spark through her, but she doused it. What was going on? Once again... brother of her ex? Hello?

"You're back in town." Allaire immediately congratulated herself on announcing the obvious. Everyone knew that Grant Clifton and Riley Douglas had asked D.J. to open one of his celebrated barbecue restaurants up at Thunder Canyon Resort. She just hadn't realized he would be here at the high school, not when there was so much to be done.

"I thought it might be time for a longer homecoming than the last visit," he said.

They held gazes and, just when the contact seemed to go on a moment too long, Allaire glanced away, holding her papers tighter against her chest. There'd been something in his eyes, something that she couldn't understand. An intensity.

Had that always been there, too?

As if to erase the tension, D.J. offered his hand in greeting. Something an acquaintance might do. Something far less intimate than what she thought she'd seen in his gaze.

She reached out to clasp his hand, wondering exactly why it was they couldn't hug hello this time. But she knew. Life hadn't only put a lot of miles and years between them—it'd taken something away, too. Something they used to share with such ease.

His hand was large, roughened by work, though she knew his job couldn't entail all that much hard labor.

Nope, he'd made a small fortune by opening a slew of D.J.'s Rib Shacks across the U.S., meaning he probably spent more time behind a desk crunching numbers than anything.

A wealthy businessman. *Her* D.J.—the studious kid who'd been too bashful to ask anyone to the prom. At the reminder of how much things *had* changed, Allaire shifted, suddenly more uncomfortable than ever.

Still, as warmth from his hand suffused her skin, her stomach heated, melting to places she'd denied herself the pleasure of using for quite some time now.

Confused at her reaction, she decided to deal with things the easy way: to be the twenty-seven-year-old paragon of wonderfulness everyone expected. The bright, optimistic, open girl who'd pretty much deserted her, although Allaire still tried to make the world think she was that same person.

"Dalton James Traub," she said, embarking on easy conversation. "What brings you to our esteemed Thunder Canyon High?"

One of D.J.'s eyebrows quirked, as if noting her sudden personality split. "Straight to business it is, then."

"Sorry. It's only that I never expected… I thought you might be busy up at the resort overseeing construction and design of the restaurant."

"After you heard the news that I was coming back, you must've known you'd see me."

"Actually," she said, "I wasn't sure I'd ever really see you again."

Guilt seemed to swipe across his features. His jaws bunched, a muscle ticking in one of them.

The blare of brass instruments saved him from having to answer as the band pivoted in their direction. D.J. nodded his head toward the football field, clearly asking her to walk with him there. He even relieved her of her workload, easily taking her bound pile of papers as if he were holding her schoolbooks at his side.

Out of old, old habit, she fell into step with him. He'd obviously not forgotten how he needed to shorten his stride to match hers, seeing as she only came up to his shoulder.

They walked down a hill, and the band's show tune softened into the background. Allaire thought that this might be the perfect opportunity for D.J. to answer her blunt comment about never seeing him again, but he didn't. No, he had always been the best listener and the best philosophical conversationalist, yet Allaire knew all too well he had always kept a part of himself sheltered.

As he was doing now.

"I thought I might come out here to ask you a favor," he said, peering into the near distance to scan the new football stadium that'd been constructed over the summer. "Well, not a favor so much as to lay out a proposition."

Proposition. The word sent naughty jabs down her body, especially since D.J. was the last one she should be making mental innuendos about.

The sensations stopped in her belly, tingling, but she folded her arms and tried to press the awareness into obscurity.

"A proposition, huh?" she said, glancing at him sidelong as they continued their stroll. She wanted to ask him why he hadn't offered any propositions over the years, why he'd kept to himself all that time.

But she knew D.J. well enough to realize he would get around to it—if he intended to address the subject at all. No use scaring him off with accusations and hard questions right now. She liked the idea of having him around again too much to blow it.

He was grinning, coming off as much more confident than ever. And why not? He was rich now, even though his modest coat, jeans and boots hardly made him out to be a wealthy man.

"Here's my thought," D.J. said. "I've seen the sets you've done for the dinner theater… what are they calling that burlesque show that's split the town down the middle opinion-wise?"

"Thunder Canyon Cowboys."

Allaire felt herself flush while referring to the gauche tourist-pleasing production that had premiered after the gold rush. A spread of riches, Thunder Canyon now attracted out-of-towners like flies to a banquet: jet-setters who descended on the resort, as well as curiosity seekers who wanted to check out the town's Old West appeal. The resort itself had been operational for almost a year, yet that didn't mean the locals had accepted the evolving status quo. *Thunder Canyon Cowboys* was just one of many flashpoints dividing the populace: those who embraced the new prosperity and those who didn't.

"You've seen the show?" Allaire asked, cringing at the notion of D.J. sitting through its corniness.

"I…took a peek." His smile told her he hadn't lasted long. "And I found out you'd done the artwork, which was definitely the best thing about it. Really impressive, Allaire. Not that I'm surprised."

Now she was feeling prideful. And why not? She'd labored hard on those set pieces, although she couldn't say she'd put her entire heart into them. Lately, she'd found it impossible to commit that much to a project. It'd been far easier when she was young and full of dreams.

"So that brings me to my proposition," D.J.

added. "I was hoping you might consider painting a mural inside the Rib Shack."

She stopped walking, stunned, and it wasn't because of his request. It was more that he was reaching out to her, even after her disastrous marriage to his brother. Shouldn't he keep avoiding her, especially because of her failure to make Dax happy?

"Of course," he continued, "you'd be well compensated. I also understand you would need to keep freelance hours because of school."

"I..." What should she say? She was still trying to figure out why D.J. had shown up out of the blue to ask her this in spite of how they'd lost touch.

As she searched for a response, the football team jogged past, their practice uniforms dirt-caked. Players called out greetings to her, and she couldn't help noticing a few students giving her the "You *go,* Ms. Traub" look as they noted D.J.

Their scrutiny embarrassed Allaire, made her too aware of how everyone in the core community would be talking because she was standing here with a man. She knew that behind her back their tongues were *already* on fire with mention of how she'd utterly failed in marriage. How she'd shamed herself with a divorce. How Allaire Traub née Buckman, an overachiever in her youth, had been expected to do much greater things with her life.

She especially couldn't bring on more gossip by getting close to her ex's brother. No doubt it would cause everyone to wonder if she was making a move on the second sibling after messing up with the first.

She could hear it now. *The girl's plowing her way through those Traub boys, isn't she?*

Sure, she knew D.J. was just offering her a job, and that was a separate issue. But the mere thought of opening herself up to speculation was too much. Her life had gotten comfortable lately, so why ruin that?

"I can't take you up on your offer," Allaire said to D.J., her heart slowing to a painful throb. "I appreciate it, but you'll have to find someone else to create that mural."

As his shoulders slumped, she wished she could tell her old best friend why.

D.J. felt as if he had been slammed by the world's largest hammer.

Damn it, he'd hoped that seeing Allaire

again wouldn't be like this. He'd spent half a lifetime running from his unrequited love for her, and he'd actually believed he'd worked her out of his system.

But the second he'd seen her across the parking lot, it was as if no time had passed at all—she was still so beautiful, with her *Alice-in-Wonderland* hair styled in an artful, spiky bun held together with two of her smaller paintbrushes. Her figure still small and slender, even under the long, bohemian-stitched sweater covering a black turtleneck, a skirt and boots. Her china-blue eyes and porcelain skin.

She was just as he remembered except, now, there were shadows in her gaze. And D.J. knew how they'd gotten there.

His brother could go to hell for hurting her.

Naturally, Allaire would never know how much D.J. resented Dax, both for the divorce as well as for everything that had led up to it. Yes, charming, bad-boy Dax had recognized Allaire's incredible qualities when he'd been a senior and D.J. and she had been juniors. But, for D.J., falling for Allaire had come much sooner because he'd been smitten ever since grade school, after brainy Allaire had moved up two grades into his own.

She'd always carried herself with an air of maturity, and D.J. had never minded that she was a couple of years younger. Consequently, they'd grown up together, his affection intensifying by the year.

Yet he'd never made a move.

Not with his best friend.

And when Dax moved in it'd been too late. The pair became the school's royal couple and, even though D.J. had always waited in the wings, telling himself he'd be there when love-'em-and-leave-'em Dax inevitably broke Allaire's heart with his carelessness, they'd stayed together. In fact, they'd gotten engaged after Allaire's graduation.

Then, just when D.J.'s heart hadn't had any pieces left to be broken, she'd asked him to be their best man.

Normally, D.J. wouldn't have refused her anything, ever, yet this was different. When he'd gracefully tried to get out of the wedding, she'd begged him to reconsider. Like the good guy he was, he'd broken down, then agreed, leaving her none the wiser as to his feelings. Smiling through the ceremony and acting the part of happy brother-in-law had left him with wounds he'd struggled to heal by returning to college at the University of Georgia and creating a life that didn't include his brother and new wife.

From that point on, it had been too painful for D.J. to return to live in Thunder Canyon, as he'd always planned. Strange, because he'd pictured himself coming back as a man who'd made himself into someone Dax could never be—truly the *best* man. In D.J.'s mind, he would win Allaire over once she recovered from the rejection he was *still* sure Dax would deal out. But the marriage had endured, which meant D.J.'s part in Allaire's life was over.

So he'd stayed in Atlanta and directed his energies to making good on his business degree. He'd become wealthy by first working at a barbecue joint for pocket change, then experimenting with his own recipe for rib sauce.

The rest was history, until Riley Douglas and the gang—Grant, Marshall, Mitchell and Russ—had persuaded him to open a Rib Shack at the resort.

D.J. had resisted at first, recalling how agonizing it had been to see Allaire at his dad's funeral, even if he had been grateful his brother had had someone to stand by his side and comfort him. However, D.J. had eventually realized that he was over Allaire now, five years later. It was about time, too. So he'd taken his friends up on their offer, returning to Thunder Canyon as a better man than he'd left…

But at this moment, in the aftermath of Allaire's latest rejection, D.J. realized that maybe he still wasn't good enough.

As they stood silently on the grass of the high school that had brought so many good times to their lives, D.J. called upon the confidence he had developed as a wildly successful businessman. *You didn't come out here to win over Allaire, you idiot. You came here to hire an artist for the Shack. Don't take her refusal personally.*

Just as their extravagantly tense pause got to the point of absurd, D.J. forced a grin. "Sorry to hear you can't do it. You were my first choice."

Always his first choice.

She dug the toe of her boot into the grass, her arms folded over her chest. "I do want to take it on, but it's…" She exhaled, then looked him in the eye.

It was a shock to his system, one that had never lost its surge.

"Is this about Dax?" he asked gently, hiding his anger with his older brother. He'd become a pro at that early on. "What would he have to say?"

"It's not what he'd have to say. It's that I... we might seem...disrespectful, maybe." She paused. "It might be insensitive of me to spend a lot of time with you when he and I don't even talk anymore."

They didn't talk anymore. That's what the gang had told D.J., too. Funny how people, whether they were ex-lovers or ex-friends, just retreated when things got too awful to bear. But it didn't sound like Dax's style to fade into any background.

Allaire continued. "Sometimes I'll see him across the Super-Save Mart or on the street. He's lost his swagger, D.J., and I don't want to add to that."

A warped part of D.J. hit on an irony: while in Atlanta, *he* had gained the confidence Dax must have misplaced. Weirder still, Thunder Canyon seemed to be sucking it right back out of D.J., too.

It gave him no joy to know his brother probably had shadows in his eyes, just like Allaire. D.J. had always hated the part of himself that envied Dax his breezy good looks and charisma, both inherited from their dad and missing from the much more reserved younger son of the family.

There'd only been one time—after Dax had suffered that near-fatal accident—that D.J. had almost let go of his resentment. Seeing Dax out cold on the hospital bed, so weak, had almost dissolved all the years of alienation and hard feelings.

Almost. When the doctor had told D.J. that Dax would be okay, D.J. had left just as secretively as he'd come in, unwilling to put his wounded brother through the distress D.J.'s presence would have no doubt caused.

"Allaire," he said, "I can understand why you'd feel that way about respecting Dax."

"You can?"

"Sure. You've always been sensitive to how others feel. But Dax can take care of himself. I doubt he's going around thinking about how his every action is affecting your opinion."

When her eyes darkened, D.J. wanted to smack himself. He hadn't meant to insinuate that she was entirely out of Dax's mind. How could *anyone* forget her?

Yet he couldn't say that out loud, not without giving himself away and risking another sure rejection.

"What I meant," he said, "is that he's probably trying to get on with life."

She laughed shortly. "You don't have to sugarcoat it, D.J. He's moved on after four years, all right. And…well, so have I. I never would've agreed to a divorce if I'd still loved him like a wife should."

Again, a terrible part of him—a part he wanted to disown—lightened at the news that she didn't feel for Dax anymore.

If that was even true.

But something about the ingenuous way Allaire watched D.J. told him that she really didn't have any emotion left for his brother.

Then again…

God, he needed to stop thinking about how she still might be drawn to Dax.

He shoved his free hand into his coat pocket. All he wanted to do was go to her, touch her. Damn it, he really hadn't gotten over her at all, had he? And here she was, more ignorant than ever as to how he felt.

Was he really putting himself through this again? Had he returned to Thunder Canyon to be that same old "nice guy" who'd never stepped up to take what he wanted?

Of course not. He was a respected businessman, a success story. This lovesick adolescent boy stuff was going to disappear any second now.

Any second.

In the silence, Allaire offered him a tiny smile—a hint of devilishness on the face of an angel—and D.J. went liquid.

Damn it.

"The thing is," she said softly, "I really missed you. Missed our old talks. Missed how we could sit around and never even *have* to talk. I've missed having you in my life."

He tried to barricade himself against her, but it was useless. Still, he found himself assuming the old D.J.'s way of fooling her, of being that steady, loyal, nonthreatening best friend who just stood back while everyone else went after their heart's desire. The kid who knew all too well how it felt to be left behind.

"I missed you, too, Allaire."

Had he ever.

"So," she said, her smile widening, even though it was still tentative, "since I can't be hanging around your restaurant for hours and hours, would you want to drop by after Open-School Night tomorrow so we can catch up?"

In public, he thought. A safe meeting.

She added, "I'd really like to spend more time chatting tonight, but I've got to do some touchups on the *Thunder Canyon Cowboys* set before the performance and then hole up with work. How about it?"

"I'll be there," he said, once more finding that he was helpless to deny her what she wanted.

The best friend. The nice guy.

They went on to small talk about her parents and how they were doing, about her teaching and how she liked it, about changes the gold rush had brought to Thunder Canyon. Then, after reminding him that she had to get to the dinner theater before tonight's seating, Allaire told him the best time to meet her tomorrow, and D.J. walked her to her Jeep.

In the meantime, he ripped into himself for falling back into the same waiting-in-the-wings buddy he'd tried to leave behind. Nothing had changed between him and Allaire, and nothing ever would.

Yet when he got into his pickup and chanced a look in the rearview mirror, his heart flared.

Allaire was still standing outside her Jeep, an expression on her face that he'd never seen before.

An expression he couldn't even begin to decipher.

A flicker of hope remained, lighting him up as she got into her car and drove off.

Chapter Two

"It was just...*off*," Allaire said while touching up a painted stream on a background piece for *Thunder Canyon Cowboys*.

Tori had gotten restless while evaluating her essays at her apartment and had joined Allaire at the empty dinner theater.

"What do you mean by *off*?" she asked, a soy-cheese-and-tomato sandwich muffling her words as she sat at a table near the stage. Both she and Allaire had been experimenting with vegetarianism the past couple of months, ever since they'd met while prepping their classrooms during the summer. Little by little, the outgoing "new teacher" had encouraged Allaire to come out of the shell she'd built around herself after the divorce.

"I mean seeing D.J. again was a very different experience." Allaire stepped away from the backdrop to survey her work, brush poised in her hand. "He didn't seem like…you know… the old D.J. so much anymore. But then again, he *did*. Does that make any sense?"

"No."

Allaire turned back around to find her friend keenly surveying her while leaning back in her faux-buffalo hide chair. Around her, the pre-performance theater stood in dim Old West spectacle, wagon-wheel chandeliers hovering, washboards, saddles and moose heads hanging on the dark plank walls. Large, round shellacked tables stood ready for the beans-and-beef dinners they'd soon be holding. In the meantime, the scent of old wood, must, campfire grub and paint all combined to create an evocative mélange.

Tori was shaking her head. "Allaire, Allaire…"

"What?"

Her friend raised her hands, sandwich and all. "Are you serious? You really didn't get the dynamics of what was going on this afternoon? Yeesh. *I* took off and left you two alone when I felt the first couple of vibrations shake the air. So obvious."

Allaire realized that this was a pivotal moment: she could either open her ears to what Tori was about to say—something she already knew herself but didn't necessarily want to acknowledge—or she could turn right back around and keep painting herself into the same corner she'd been in for the past ten years or so. A corner filled with frustrated ambitions and torched dreams.

She lifted her eyebrows, inviting Tori to go on.

"You aren't kids anymore," her friend said. "And the two of you realize it, but it seems too weird or…something. You don't fulfill the same niches in each other's lives, but it's too discomfiting for you to adjust your lenses."

Oh, but Allaire had done just that when she'd first seen D.J. in the parking lot. She'd noticed his broader shoulders, a face that had gained more of what a person might call "character." She'd never understood what that meant, but seeing D.J. today defined it. His eyes spoke of years spent away from his hometown, his skin grown rougher—a man's shadow-stubbled complexion in lieu of a boy's baby-smooth one.

At the thought, her stomach flip-flopped, and she barred an arm over it. What would everyone think if they knew D.J. had caught her eye?

"One Traub boy wasn't enough?"

And she could just hear what Arianna, her older sister, would say. "Why even bother getting involved at all? Love rots."

However, the worst part would be in having to face her parents. Sure, her mom and dad could handle the small-town gossip with their normal good grace, but Allaire would know what they were thinking all the same. They would silently wonder where their perfect little girl had gone wrong, why she wasn't as successful in love as she'd been in algebra or literature or her art electives. They would never say a word, yet Allaire would know, deep down, that she'd disappointed them, just as she'd done when she had gotten divorced.

"So," Tori said, commanding Allaire's attention, "tell me you're not going to pretend that you didn't see it, too. I swear, Allaire, wake up and smell the cupid."

"Smell the cupid?"

"Or…whatever. Don't change the subject. It's not such a bad thing to be interested in someone, you know. Getting divorced didn't put a scarlet letter on your chest."

"They didn't put any kind of mark on me that I didn't earn."

"What are you, perfect? You'd be the only one."

The other woman set her sandwich on her brown-bag wrapping. "You can't give them the power to dictate your life."

"I…don't." But, oh, she sure did. She'd been born and raised in this town, watched over by the community and held to their expectations. She hadn't minded, either, because she'd intended to surpass every marker they'd laid out for her, every goal.

Allaire wandered over to rest her paintbrush, then hopped off the stage and joined Tori at the table.

"D.J. was my *best friend*." She reached for her quilted hobo bag and riffled through it for a padded photo case. When she opened it, she smiled at D.J. and Dax's senior pictures. Both were in spiffy suits, Dax looking suave in a smooth matinee-idol way, D.J. looking like he'd rather be yanking off his tie and ducking out of the frame.

"Wow. This is your ex?" Tori said, pointing to Dax.

No surprise—she'd fixated on the elder brother first. Next to Dax, D.J. had always disappeared into the woodwork.

So what had changed about him? Was it maturity that had given him more of an edge, an alluring quality?

"That's Dax, all right," Allaire said. "He owns the motorcycle shop near the Clip 'n' Curl. He used to race professionally. Doesn't he look the part?"

"Allaire, you have good taste."

Allaire shrugged, but her friend had already moved on to inspect D.J.'s photo.

"Aw," she said. "The boy next door."

At that, Allaire's heart sank a little. She and D.J. had lost so much, and she wished she knew how to get it back. You didn't find friends like him growing on trees.

But what if they could piece their relationship back together? Hadn't today been a start?

Couldn't it be the same, even with everything that'd happened after high school?

"Seems to me," Tori said, "that you outgrew Dax and found D.J. today."

A sense of panic—or maybe it was the shock of truth—zapped Allaire. "Wrong. Even if your appraisal held any grain of truth, I'd never date the brother of an ex-husband. It'd be awkward, to say the least."

"Are you still in love with Dax or something? Because that's not what you've been telling me every time I want to go to The Hitching Post on a Friday night."

Allaire was already shaking her head. "I don't love him anymore—not in that way. There's still a…fondness, I suppose. We don't hate each other. There aren't even hard feelings. Our marriage was like one of those songs that doesn't have a real ending, if that makes sense. It kind of repeated over and over until it faded to nothing."

Tori was cocking her head, fully invested, urging Allaire to go on.

"Dax and I started dating in high school, and our feelings really were genuine. You know how it is when you're younger. At that point, real life hasn't intruded much. There aren't any big compromises to be made yet. And we didn't live with each other before the wedding, though we did get married shortly after high school. I gave up all the plans I'd made, like going to a state college and studying art in Europe. Those things didn't matter at the time. I loved Dax and that was top priority."

"And you got resentful eventually."

Allaire wasn't so sure it was resentment as much as regret. "Sometimes young love doesn't mature very well, and that was what happened with us. When I was a girl, I was this…I guess you could say 'fragile dreamer.' And when it turned out that I had a buried independent streak—something I hadn't been very aware of—Dax balked. Not that I blame him. He'd been expecting a wife who would devote her time to being with him on the racing circuit, and that lost its shine for me pretty quickly."

"Understandable. So while Dax raced, did you start pursuing those old ambitions? Did you go over to Europe for some studying?"

"I wish." She'd still been Dax's wife, keeping the home fires burning. "But I did pursue an art education on a different scale. I decided that by going back to school and getting a teaching credential, I could still live a few dreams through my students. I mean, teaching—what a job, right? I'd get to share my love of art while creating some of it on my own, too. But Dax didn't see it that way because he wanted me to cheer him on in every race. One night when he was off-circuit, he said I'd become a stranger, because I hadn't minded being his pep club before. I took exception to that and asked him if he seriously thought I was just going to remain the same compliant dreamer I had been in school."

Even now, that particular epiphany surprised her. It'd taken years for her to develop, yet so many things had stayed the same. She was still too worried about what others thought, and though she was much more sensible now-adays, she would always have a heart prone to dreaming.

That's why she spent so much time doing freelance work besides her teaching, balancing the fantasy with the reality as she avoided having to face hard questions about life.

"Darlin'—" Tori leaned over the table to place a hand on Allaire's arm "—you still might have a lot of sweet and fragile in you, but there's the heart of a lion beneath it all."

Allaire smiled, wondering if that were true,

especially as she rested her gaze on the stage-bound set pieces.

She didn't see much heart in her work at all.

The next night, D.J. made sure he wrapped up his meetings with the Rib Shack contractors on time and was out the door before the clock struck eight. Allaire had told him that she'd almost be done greeting her students and parents by that hour.

And D.J. wanted her all to himself.

As he parked his pickup in the lot, he told himself not to get excited. First of all, other teachers would still be around as de facto chaperones. Second of all, he shouldn't expect her to suddenly realize she'd made a mistake in marrying Dax and run to him instead. He knew his old friend better than that. Both of them realized Dax would be standing between them, no matter how hard D.J. might hope that she really saw *him*—the man who'd been waiting for her to notice—and not his brother.

He walked into the school's side entrance, moving past a rainbowed sign that said Open-School Night! Allaire had told him that she was based in Mr. Richard's old classroom, so D.J. headed straight there. Funny how he still recalled these locker-lined halls, even with the changes—a new wing of classrooms, a revamped office area. Even the same stale school air lingered.

When he found Allaire leaning against a wall and chatting with another teacher, he almost tripped over his own boots. His pulse threaded in and out of itself in a demented race.

Her pale hair was up in that spiky bun again, and she was dressed in a beige suit with black piping that reminded him of a Victorian woman. Even her shoes were those black ankle boots that buttoned up the side.

She was his every fantasy, right here, in the flesh, and D.J. didn't know if he had it in him to ever claim her.

But, again, he hadn't come back to Thunder Canyon for Allaire. When he'd left, he'd promised himself that he would return only when he truly became a man worthy of winning her, and he wasn't sure when he'd get to that point. Or if he ever would. Besides, it wasn't in D.J. to disrespect Dax by taking up with his former wife. Even though D.J. and his sibling hadn't spoken much over the years—only via phone calls when Dad had passed from a heart attack—they were still related. Still bonded by family, although D.J. hardly felt the connection.

When Allaire spotted him, he could've sworn that she was affected, too. Her gaze locked with his, digging into him until his heart blasted against his breastbone, chiseling at it.

Then she stood away from the wall, sending him a cool smile that had him wondering if he'd imagined the moment.

He took that as a hint to approach, his boot steps echoing off the walls like beats of a clock going backward in time.

Nodding at the older female brunette next to Allaire, D.J. said, "I'd forgotten how this place smelled."

The brunette laughed. "Teenaged bodies. Sweat, perfume and a general sense of wildness."

"Smoke, too," D.J. added.

"From the bathrooms." Allaire gestured down the hall, where a banner advertised the homecoming dance in pink-glitter glory. "We do our best to monitor, but it's not always good enough."

Quickly, she introduced D.J. to Mrs. Steph,

the PE teacher and softball coach. Then the other woman excused herself, eager to get home to her family.

"Looks like the place cleared out," he said while Allaire began walking him down the hall, away from her closed classroom.

"We got a rush around six-thirty. Now everyone's in the family room watching primetime TV, I suppose."

Her talk was light, casual, but the ghosts of old kept thickening every word, weighting them with far more than she probably intended.

"You giving me a tour?" he asked, trying diligently to keep himself in check. But all he wanted to do was reach out—just one time— and touch her hair. He imagined it'd be as soft as the shampoo she'd always used: a lavender concoction. Yet now there was a certain kick to the scent that hadn't existed before. It drew him until he had to fight himself back.

"A tour was the plan." She grinned up at him, and it was as if they were back ten years, him walking her to physics or U.S. history. "You haven't seen the new cafeteria yet. It's our pride and joy."

"Must be a trip for you to see how things change before your eyes here. It's weird enough for me. All the benches and windows seem really small now."

"Perspective, D.J. How can you not see things differently when you've come back here as a millionaire?"

The term struck him as uncomfortable. "I wouldn't go that far."

Allaire shot him a curious glance. "Why not? You're almost a Horatio Alger story—a kid who went to seek his fortune in a big city, apprenticing, then discovering he had a real knack for the restaurant business."

Honestly, D.J. considered his success to be a bit ludicrous, his swollen bank account obscene. He'd never thought making so much money doing something he loved to be possible. But he'd paid a price, and the cost had been losing touch with the woman he'd secretly loved.

"Honestly," he said, "I'm still not used to it all."

She smiled, more to herself than him, really. "That's not surprising. You were never flashy."

Not like Dax.

Though the thought went unsaid, it was there, a solid specter.

She seemed to realize it, too. Flipping the

subject, she said, "I'll bet you have to pinch yourself every once in a while as a reminder that you can afford fine things, huh?"

She'd hit the nail on the head, as usual. No one else had ever come close to understanding his every thought. Still, she would never guess that he wished he could use his money to fulfill all those dreams Allaire had treasured in high school: moving to Paris to study the exhibits in the Louvre with all the time and care this would require, setting up an easel on the banks of the Seine to paint the sunset over the water.

But none of that mattered anymore. It couldn't. Hell, even if D.J. ever summoned the courage to tell her how he felt—or, he told himself, how he *used* to feel—about her, he would always wonder if she was seeing him as the runner-up to the dashing Dax.

D.J. didn't want to be her consolation prize, especially since he'd spent a lifetime being second best to his sibling—with Allaire, and even with D.J.'s own dad.

When they reached the cafeteria, which was locked for the night, she peeked through the windows, clearly not recognizing that she was tearing D.J. apart.

"Come here." She waved him to her side.

He hesitated, then obliged her. Her scent filled him up, made him dizzy.

"They put in a food court," she said. "Don't you wish we'd had something like that way back when?"

D.J. didn't give a hang about the cafeteria.

He must've taken much too long to answer, because she peered up at him, her soft lips shaped as if to ask a question. Yet she stopped before a sound came out. Then, almost imperceptibly, she put distance between them. It wasn't even physical space: it was far more devastating because it was mental, emotional.

"I wish you hadn't gone to Atlanta," she finally said.

What could he say? *I left because, at your wedding, I wanted to die, Allaire. I couldn't stand to see you pledging yourself to Dax when I should've been the one standing with you at the altar instead.*

But voicing that wasn't in anyone's best interests. However, there was another reason he'd left, one he'd never told her. Maybe now was as good a time as any to do it since the anguish wasn't so immediate anymore.

"I'd had enough here in Thunder Canyon," he said. "Enough of a lot of things."

"Like…what?" She looked as if she regretted bringing up the subject, but there was something about her that seemed to egg him on, too, as if she *wanted* him to come clean.

Hell, that was probably just a wish begging for fulfillment.

"When we were kids," he said, "you might've noticed that Dax and I weren't that close. I'm guessing it became even more obvious after you married."

Allaire turned to lean against the cafeteria window. At the same time, she kept a chasm between them.

"I suspected that you two weren't bonded. I never knew why, though."

"That's because we never enjoyed what you might call a 'buddy-buddy' relationship."

Allaire frowned, processing something in that quick mind of hers. He'd missed watching her think.

"See," she said, "I would've expected you two to be close after your mom died when you were so young."

Maybe it should've been that way. When Mom had gotten in that accident out near the bypass, Dax had been eleven, D.J. ten.

"It happened the opposite way," he said, noticing that his voice held a note of latent pain. Maybe this was all much closer to the surface than he'd thought. "Instead of bonding with each other in the aftermath, we went into our own personal caves. I became studious, Dax became interested in his motorcycles, just like Dad. They would work together, night after night, not saying anything, but you could tell it made them feel better. It gave them solace."

"And that put you out in the cold. Oh, D.J., I never realized that."

"I never told you. Besides, it's all in the past."

The lie tasted foreign on D.J.'s tongue, and he realized that he'd never graduated from the profound sense of isolation that had resulted from being ignored by his dad and brother. He wasn't about to admit that their bond had made him envious. He'd worked too damned hard to overcome it, and just because he was willing to let Allaire in on some explanations didn't mean she would get any others.

It was best to hide his resentment toward Dax for stealing their father's attention when their mother had so recently been snatched from their lives, too. D.J. didn't even like to recognize this acrimony in himself, and his unwillingness to face it had caused the hard feelings to escalate, then fester when Dax had won Allaire's affections.

D.J. had been the odd man out in so many ways, but he'd always tried to master the complex. All the same, he kept hating himself for never having the bravado to step up and claim the woman he loved, just as he should've stepped up to claim his dad's attention, also. What made things so much worse, though, was that D.J. knew that he—and he alone—was responsible for all this fruitless pining.

So that's why he'd tried to become a new man.

A person he could be proud of again.

Chapter Three

Allaire watched the emotions play across D.J.'s face. His cheeks, leaner and hungrier than when he was young, tensed as he clenched his jaw. His eyes were dark and unreadable.

This didn't feel right, his shutting her out.

"I think I get what you're saying about your relationship with Dax," she said. "No one wants to be stranded to fend for themselves emotionally. It wasn't fair that they cut you out of their inner circle after your mom died, but I'm sure they didn't realize what was happening."

"You're right."

His tone was weary, and she didn't sense bitterness as much as acknowledgment. And when he sighed, then walked away, she wondered just what else D.J. had been hiding from her all these years. Had she really known her best friend that well?

Maybe she should've made it a point to find out why D.J. and Dax had always seemed civilly distant with each other, even if they'd hung out with the same group. She'd just assumed that, even with the subtle tension between them, they still had a bond, like siblings were supposed to. In her experience, she'd enjoyed a close, if sometimes strained, relationship with her own much older sister and, true to naive form, Allaire had assumed that was how it was for most families.

But after marrying Dax, she couldn't remember ever hearing the brothers talk on the phone or seeing them exchange an e-mail—not until their dad died, anyway. And even then their communication had been brief and to the point.

A couple of times, she'd asked Dax to elaborate, but he'd told her that he and D.J. were men, and how many men spent hours on the phone gabbing to each other? With a heavy feeling, she hadn't pursued the subject. Her marriage was already weak at that point, and this was the least of their issues.

However, now wasn't the time for pursuing the truth with D.J., either, so she caught up with him, bumping against his arm as a tacit way of saying she understood that he wanted to drop the subject.

The second she felt the hard muscle, even through his coat and her suit, Allaire's skin came alive. Heat zinged through her chest, downward, zapping neglected areas and settling there.

She crossed her arms, wishing the sensations would go away. Wishing they would stay.

Soon, the two of them came to the gym, which was already chained shut. Even so, she seized the chance to look through a window, just as she had at the cafeteria when she'd been searching for anything to avoid the confusion D.J. was conjuring inside of her.

He came up behind her. She could feel the warmth of him, feel his breath stroking the back of her exposed neck.

"Old Mr. Ozzel," she said, referring to the elderly custodian who was dust-mopping the gym's shiny wooden floor. "Remember him?"

D.J.'s laugh softly chopped through Allaire. Her nape tingled, prickling the rest of her skin to goose bumps.

What was happening here?

"How could I forget him?" D.J. asked. "That night when you and I were leaving late because of a journalism deadline? Ozzel thought we were up to no good, wandering the halls with a mind to vandalize, so he hid himself and then yelled that we needed to scram or he'd '*git* us.'"

Allaire laughed, even though, at the time, she'd been scared of getting in trouble. Such a good girl. "We didn't know it was Mr. Ozzel at first, so I ran, and you came after me because I was escalating the situation. He was fast on your tail, waving his mop. But he wouldn't have caught us if you hadn't come to your senses and turned around to make peace with him." She laughed. "You were so well mannered, D.J., even in the face of catastrophe."

She remembered it all now. D.J. the peacemaker, the levelheaded nice guy who smoothed out each and every hairy situation.

Except, obviously, his own home life....

"I tell you," she said, her old affection for him feeling new again, "Mr. Ozzel became

your number-one fan that night when you han-
dled everything so…how did he say?"

"So like a wise sorcerer who's out to calm
a fire-breathing dragon. Ozzel was way into
his fantasy novels."

"That remains the same." She smiled, still
facing away from D.J. It gave her the courage
to voice what she said next. "I think Mr. Ozzel
wanted to marry you off to his daughter because you were such a catch. A lot of the girls
thought so, too. Just how is it that you managed to avoid being roped in by someone in
Atlanta, D.J.?"

She heard his breathing hitch, and heat lined
her belly.

Turning her head slightly, still not looking
at him, she fished some more. "You did date
there."

Shame on her for asking, but she wanted to
know. Needed to know for some indefinable
reason.

He cleared his throat, sending a cascade
down her body.

"You first, nosey," he said.

"All right." No biggie. "I haven't had much
interest in 'playing the game,' as Tori might
say, since the divorce."

At his silence, she continued. "I know, I know, I need to start, but…I'm not enthused about trying. Not right now."

He waited, as if anticipating that she would go on. But there was nothing to add. Zip. Bo-o-o-oring.

At that moment, Mr. Ozzel saw her peering through the window, and he raised a hand from the handle of his dust mop and waved.

She returned the gesture. "And you, Romeo?"

In spite of her flippancy, his voice lowered. "I dated all right. But there was never…anyone."

"Anyone?" *Clam up, Allaire. It's not really any of your business.*

"What can I say?" He laughed, but it sounded almost too jovial. "No one could ever measure up to you, Allaire."

Her heartbeat yanked and tangled, blood stopping in its flow, leaving her light-headed. But was it because she hadn't wanted D.J. to say something so blunt?

Or because she had?

When he laughed again, less forcefully this time, she turned all the way around, coming face-to-chest with him. She raised her chin to look up at her old friend, just to see if he was truly joking around.

Time suspended in suddenly thickened air. A flash of something—*what?*—filled his dark gaze, and his lips parted as if to speak.

Allaire found herself holding her breath, eyes widening. Instinct told her that he was about to turn her world on its ear, and she didn't know if she could withstand the change. Not after she'd failed so miserably in her first marriage, not after she'd disappointed her-self—and her family—so spectacularly.

Besides, this was D.J. *D.J.*—the one guy who would never threaten her heart.

As if reading her, D.J. pressed his lips to-gether, then averted his gaze as he backed away, hands stuffed in his coat pockets.

Breathless, Allaire couldn't move for a mo-ment. What had that been about?

Did she even want to know?

She didn't think so. More than anything, she wanted a friend again. She'd missed his com-panionship so much, and now she had the op-portunity to reclaim it.

He headed back to her classroom, shoul-ders stiff. Luckily, two of Allaire's colleagues strolled past, breaking the tension with cheerful good-nights and see-you-tomorrows.

By the time they got back to her room, D.J. had loosened up. She almost would've guessed nothing had transpired back at the gym doors but for the way her heart was still jammed in her throat.

At the threshold of her closed door, he sent her a very D.J.-like grin: soothing, sweet. The type of smile moms and dads all over the heartland loved to see on the faces of a neighborhood boy.

Heck, she'd been creating monsters out of shadows, hadn't she? D.J. hadn't meant anything back by the gym. He'd truly been joking around.

"In the end," he said, jerking his chin toward her door, "I really can't leave without at least seeing what you've been up to. You ready to show off?"

Suddenly shy, she meandered past him to unlock the door. Warmth flooded her yet again.

Okay, that really needed to stop.

"You asked for it." She pushed open the door. "Enter at your own risk."

She gauged his reaction, hoping for approval, as always. But with D.J., it was as if she were taking him to a favorite viewpoint on a mountain or reading him a poem that had touched her. Although her classroom was public, it was also a private treasure: a place where she and her students transferred all their dreams into art.

She realized how much D.J.'s opinion meant to her. How much it'd always meant, even though she hadn't been exposed to it for so long.

He entered, silently taking in the ordered insanity of halfway-finished tile murals, collages, paintings, drawings and sculptures. Through him, she smelled the oils and plaster, felt the cool of the air and the shiver of a creative haven.

"Damn," was all he said.

But, somehow, it meant everything. The extent of his "damn" showed in the glow of his gaze, in the way he planted his hands on his hips as if he were surveying an impressive skyline.

"It's nothing much." She wandered to her desk and shuffled through a neat pile of papers, just so she wouldn't have to show him how much his reaction affected her. "The kids work hard."

D.J. had walked over to a painting near the shuttered window: a canvas half-shrouded, leaving only a peak of blue-gray uncovered. As he lifted off the sheet, Allaire sucked in a lungful of oxygen.

He'd found it—the project she'd been laboring over since school had started.

It was an educated guess—a whimsical take—on what nighttime Paris might look like from the balcony of a modest hotel. It was a substitute for her never having traveled there, a representation of the ambitions she'd let fly into the wind after high school.

"Allaire," D.J. said softly, and she knew exactly what he was seeing because she'd described her hopes to him so many times.

Sadness, happiness, *something* tightened her throat and dampened her eyes, yet she didn't allow herself to cry. Nothing was so bad it could make her do that.

"That's how I've been letting off steam," she said carefully. "That and my freelance dinner-theater stuff."

"This…" D.J. kept staring at the painting, even if it was only the beginning of a final image. "You've matured. I always knew you had talent—everyone knew—but, damn, Allaire, what're you doing teaching in a high school?"

Ouch.

D.J. glanced at her, an apology in his gaze. "I didn't mean it that way. Teaching's noble. I was only trying to compliment you."

The honesty in his tone unsettled her. She didn't know why, but she'd never been able to deal with praise. It was much easier to believe the negative and strive to improve after that.

The curse of a people pleaser, she thought.

Her next words came out more as a dodge to hearing additional compliments than anything. "Dax said that teaching was a better idea than taking time off to study art. I mean, he told me I was good, sure, but I don't think he ever paid enough attention to my work to really see it...."

At the mention of his brother's name, D.J. had straightened, covering her painting back up.

Great. She'd had to go and open her big mouth. Why did Dax always seem to wedge himself into their conversations? D.J. obviously didn't want to talk about him, but there she was, bringing him up again.

Maybe, subconsciously, she'd even done it on purpose.

D.J. glanced at the ground, then at her. She could tell that there were no hard feelings, thank goodness. Wonderful, dependable D.J.

"I wish you'd reconsider doing that mural for me," he said. "And I'm not only offering because of the old-friend network. You'd add some beauty and substance to my place, Allaire. I mean it."

Maybe it was out of guilt for mentioning Dax, or maybe it was because she sensed D.J. genuinely did appreciate her talents. But Allaire found herself giving the idea a second thought.

A new start on a new project, she thought. But there had to be rules.

"Would I be working…alone?" she asked.

D.J. narrowed his eyes. "If you're worried about provincial gossip that might surface because you're around me, then no. I'll make sure there's always quiet work going on around you."

"Quiet." She laughed. "I'm kind of used to being surrounded by students. They work by my side unless they need guidance."

She couldn't help it. Fresh ideas were already flooding her head. Maybe this mural could even be her best effort yet. Then again, that's what she always thought before starting a new work.

"Great." D.J. rubbed his hands together. "So, as the featured artist, you'd need to clear room on your calendar for the grand Rib Shack opening. You'd be my special guest."

Thoughts of what he'd said earlier about never finding anyone as good as her rushed back. It led Allaire to a gut feeling that D.J. could be asking her to the opening as his date, so she nipped that in the bud. Or maybe she was just that neurotic. Probably.

"Just tell me when to show up and I'll be there for my buddy's big night," she said brightly.

When his smile fell, Allaire scolded herself. Had she gone too far in her effort to make things clear?

But, in the next moment, he was back to being casual, nice D.J.—the guy with the comforting grin.

"To a buddy's big night then," he said, as her heart slumped in relief.

Or maybe it had slumped in…

Jeez, she didn't even know anymore.

A week later, ten days prior to opening night, the Rib Shack was almost set to go.

They'd moved into an area where the resort had already planned to house a restaurant, so the kitchen was just about in working order. As well, the dining room's family-style tables and picnic benches were due for delivery soon. D.J. had even secured a staff, thanks to the guidance of Grant Clifton, and some of them were in back, experimenting with cooking gadgets and listening to the expertise of current employees brought over from already existing Rib Shacks. D.J. had known he could depend on Grant for anything, especially since his high school pal had played a major part in bringing this restaurant to Thunder Canyon.

Now, D.J. stood at the long bar lining the left side of the room across from where the mural would lord it over the diners. He was tinkering with the frame of one of the sepia ranch photos that would decorate the rough-pine walls. Yet, even though he was at work, he couldn't help glancing at Allaire every few seconds as she immersed herself in her art.

It was something to behold, although D.J. knew the poetry of her motion wouldn't speak to everyone. Certainly her beauty—even hidden beneath roomy overalls and a gray thermal shirt—would enthrall most. But the mere sight of Allaire tilting her head as she considered where to use a certain color was pure magic to D.J. Maybe it was because he could sense the deep thoughts going into every brushstroke… or maybe it was because he'd never been able to keep his eyes off of her anyway.

Damn it, with each of her visits, he couldn't help but to admit the truth: he'd never stopped loving her.

So, what was he going to do about it? Stand back, just as he'd done when they were younger? Was that the best choice when all he wanted to do was make her happy?

She was over Dax—he was becoming surer of that each day. From chatting with his friends while taking care to hide his true feelings, D.J. had discerned that Dax and Allaire's marriage had gradually waned. Actually, the boys said that the only reason the couple had stayed together for as long as they had was that neither person had wanted to give up. D.J. could understand this coming from both Allaire, a woman ultrasensitive to what others thought, *and* his brother. D.J. knew competitive Dax was stubborn, and a divorce would mean he hadn't won.

Or maybe there was more to it—if only D.J.

were to hear Dax's side, he wouldn't have to listen to what others were saying about him.

But neither brother had contacted the other, and that spoke louder than any chatter.

Done with the frame, D.J. went back into the kitchen, where he gave himself a break from being around Allaire. Seeing her was enough to recall Open-School Night, when she'd reminded him that they were just buddies after he'd asked her to the Shack's grand opening. That was one of the reasons he had never gotten up enough guts to ask her out pre-Dax, and the reminder hadn't exactly been encouraging.

Needing a distraction, D.J. whipped up a batch of ribs for dinner as the new line cooks gathered round.

Eventually he emerged from the back, finding Allaire on her knees, texturing a horse's hoof. The mural surrounded her with like images: cowboys, miners, even The Hitching Post—the town's old, so-called brothel-turned-bar-and-grill. The ironic parallel to the state of today's Thunder Canyon didn't escape D.J.; upon his return, it'd been a shock to see how commercial everything had become. Then again, a gold strike and a multimillion-dollar resort could do that to a place.

A few minutes later, when Allaire paused in her task, D.J. shuffled around, not wanting to sneak up on her. She jumped anyway, hand to her heart as she turned around and laughed.

"I get so caught up," she said.

"It looks perfect."

He bent to a knee, handing her a plate filled with ribs, coleslaw, home-fried potatoes and a slab of corn bread.

Allaire ran to the washroom to clean up. In the meantime, D.J. settled himself on the floor since there wasn't any furniture yet. The aroma of his sauce, slathered over the meat, made his mouth water; he hadn't eaten since an early lunch meeting with Grant.

However, when Allaire returned and made herself cozy on the plastic covering the carpet, D.J. saw that she picked right over the ribs and preferred the coleslaw. *Hmmm.* People generally went face-first into his main course.

She noticed his reaction and smiled. "Hate to break it you, but I'm a vegetarian."

He almost choked on his meal. "Since when?"

Allaire raised her gaze in thought. It was cute enough to make him forget everything and scoop her right against him.

But…he knew better. He'd been trained well.

"I believe it's been a little over a month now." Allaire made a sorry-about-that expression and nibbled on the slaw. "This is great, though."

"A month? Allaire, when we used to go to that drive-in burger joint off Main Street, weren't you the girl who wolfed down the Monster Special?"

"At Digger's?" Now she looked dreamy, as if recalling the taste of those meals they'd grabbed on the weekends. "That was me, all right." Then she seemed to remember her resolve. "But those days are over. I read *Fast Food Nation*. Do you know what goes into mass-produced beef?"

"Whoa, whoa." D.J. held up his sauce-coated hand. "I deal directly with private ranchers who have standards. That's why I serve modest food that's just upscale enough for the Thunder Canyon Resort."

He sent her a cocky grin.

"Oh, you're so cool." She took a bite of the corn bread, then closed her eyes and dramatically fell to her side. "The bread. The bread. I'm in heaven."

At pleasing her, D.J.'s chest swelled. However, his body swelled in another region altogether as she lay on the floor, smiling as if he'd just satisfied her deepest craving.

He calmed himself. *Right. Dream on.*

"Feel free to catch a wink or two while you're at it," he said.

"Maybe I will. Working these hours has been getting to me, but you know what? I wouldn't want to be doing anything else."

He knew it—art was Allaire's escape. And, from what he'd pieced together about her divorce, he realized she yearned for the freedom to fly away, even mentally.

From the floor, she grinned at him again, and he couldn't help doing the same. Yet then he realized he probably had a face full of sauce, and the moment dissolved as he reached for a packet of moistened towelettes and used one.

When he was done, Allaire pushed herself to a sitting position. "You missed a spot."

She took another towelette and moved toward him, close enough for him to breathe in her soft perfume, the lotion she used on her skin.

God…

With care, she ran the cloth under his bottom lip, and D.J.'s eyes fluttered shut in primal response. His chest throbbed, the cadence echoing low in his belly as he imagined Allaire in their house, at their dinner table taking care of him.

It should've been that way, D.J. thought. *He* should've been the one who'd courted her. He should've been the one asking Dax to be his best man, because by then, with Allaire at D.J.'s side, it would've been so much easier to find peace with his brother.

But in the next heartbeat, D.J.'s eyes had opened, and what he saw was the reality.

Allaire was watching him with wide eyes. He could see her questions, the fear that D.J. would once more step over the line of their friendship. He'd done it last week, too, at Open-School Night, when he'd told her that there'd never been anyone else like her in his life.

Yeah, he'd spun that into a joke—one he doubted Allaire bought—but it'd been the truth. And, for the first time ever, being honest about his feelings had been liberating… until he realized that Allaire probably didn't want to hear what he had to offer.

He would always be her pal.

As if to prove that, she patted his face lightly and went back to her seat.

"Want to know something?" she said.

He would've expected the world to come down around his ears after such a strained moment, but Allaire was wearing that devilish grin and he couldn't give in to the stress.

D.J. took the bait, even though she was only changing the subject again. "Shoot."

She got to her knees, canting toward the mural. "Don't hate me, but I've been doing more than just rendering cowboys here."

"Do tell."

She pointed to a darkened spot that served to transition a gold pan into a shimmering waterfall.

His gaze focused on an ethereal symbol amid the painted transition.

"Tell me that's not the Eiffel Tower," he said, leaning closer.

Allaire made a touchdown sign with her arms. "Yes! I wanted to put my personality into this. Eventually, you're going to be able to pick out my fantasy trip to Europe in the mural—iconic images like the Leaning Tower of Pisa and the Swiss Alps. But you'll have to look closely."

D.J. loved the thought of having a part of her in his restaurant. It was like a gift.

She must've taken his silence for disapproval, because immediately she seemed worried.

"Is that all right?" she asked.

He latched his gaze to hers, connecting, settling into what was more of a home than he'd ever had. "You shouldn't wonder about my opinion," he said. "I'll always appreciate your work."

And you, he tacitly added. *I'll always appreciate anything you see fit to give me.*

Her gaze brightened, as blue and vivid as the mural's waterfall, and D.J. told himself it was enough.

At least for now.

Chapter Four

Four more days passed, filled with nights that Allaire spent perfecting the Rib Shack's mural.

Nights that Allaire spent wondering what was going on between her and D.J. as he continued to oversee the last-minute details of the opening.

Whenever he was in the same room, she felt him on her skin, *under* it. But she never looked back at him. Instead, she became a part of her mural, losing herself in its fantasy.

Tonight she was working the Roman Colosseum into a red dress worn by Lily Divine, the infamous was-she-or-wasn't-she town madam back in the early days. Just a touch of shading here, a dab of texture there, and Allaire almost had it.

But then she sensed D.J., and her thoughts went up in smoke. Heat seemed to undulate in her tummy as the sound of careful bootsteps thudded to a stop behind her.

She sent an inquisitive glance over her shoulder, finding D.J. there, all right, dressed in his jeans and flannel shirt. There was nothing big-city or rich-boy about him, and when she remembered that he was a wealthy businessman, it always came as a bit of a surprise.

"Are you here to remind me to eat again?" she asked.

"Am I that predictable?"

He said it as if being constant was a bad thing. But Allaire wanted to tell him that his kind of predictable was nice, welcome, exactly what she'd been lacking in a marriage that had always seemed to shift beneath her feet.

D.J. hitched a thumb toward the rear entrance, where a man in camouflage was painting the wide door frame.

"I was thinking we could grab a bite at the Grubstake," he said, referring to the grill in the main lodge.

"Sounds good to me." Allaire stood, then went to clean up and grab a jacket before recalling that the main lodge was connected to one of two Rib Shack entrances via a hallway. But since she wasn't dressed to the nines—not even to the ones, really—she slipped her jacket over her paint-dotted shirt anyway, merely to cover up.

She and D.J. took off then, passing a corridor filled with high-end shops featuring winter wear in the windows. A few slender, coiffed women milled inside, choosing their finery with care. Open storefronts languished in between the franchises, spaces that the resort would be renting out in the future.

Allaire was fascinated. "I hadn't actually toured this place until you came along, and I never realized it'd be so much like falling down the rabbit hole."

"Yeah. Never in a million years did I predict Thunder Canyon would be the next Vail. Then again, I'm not exactly complaining since I'm a part of this new wave of progress now. It's just…unexpected. Every bit of it."

"Luckily," she said, gently punching his arm, "some things never change. Neither do some people."

D.J. didn't say much. Maybe he was thinking that everyone did change, but most just didn't want to admit it.

At the end of the corridor, the main lodge opened into bustling splendor. It had a five-story central wing in addition to the wings on either side of the sprawling yet elegantly rustic building.

Here, D.J.'s stride slowed, then stopped altogether.

"D.J.?" she asked.

His gaze was fixed on something ahead, near the entrance to the lounge, which housed a bar on one side and a coffeehouse on the other.

Dax Traub was sauntering out, tugging his leather jacket around his body as he headed for the lodge exit.

The name *James Dean* briefly flashed through Allaire's thoughts, like a flow of water sluicing through her fingers. She'd always thought her boyfriend, then husband, looked like the brooding movie icon. He had the hot-rod attitude, carefree brown hair and dark eyes to match.

But now? Now he moved like a man who didn't have much to look forward to.

Chest tight, she was surprised by how her feelings for Dax had altered. There wasn't any spark now. There was only a memory of how unsuspecting they'd both been at the beginning, then the reality of how things had actually turned out.

She turned to D.J., whose gaze was glued to his brother. His shoulders didn't have the stiffness she'd expected and, if Allaire didn't know any better, she would say her friend was tempted to go after Dax to say something. *Anything.* Did he want to break the ice that had formed between them?

"Go, D.J.," she said. "I'll get something to eat later."

For a second, it seemed as if D.J. was going to take her up on that. The muscle in his jaw loosened, and he looked…hopeful.

Yet that faded as Dax disappeared down the stairs.

Without comment, D.J. headed toward the Grubstake, clearly deciding to turn away from his brother.

Something like anger rattled Allaire. Damn that Traub stubbornness.

"You just passed up the best chance you're

going to get for a while," she said, following him into the restaurant.

As if blocking her out, he continued to the welcome podium, asked for a booth for two, then followed the hostess. The aroma of grilled meats burnished the atmosphere, lending a charred feel to the horseshoe-decorated walls.

"D.J.?" she asked, trailing him as he continued on his silent way.

They reached the leatherette booth, and he took a seat while Allaire stayed standing.

The hostess wisely retreated after depositing the menus on the table. But Allaire wasn't done.

"You've been in town for how long? About two weeks now? And I know you still haven't even called your own brother."

D.J. blew out a breath, perusing his menu. He was barely holding it together, she could tell.

Allaire let up on him. Why she thought it was her business to interfere, she didn't know. She was the ex-wife, the family friend, and that was it. But it killed her to see what was happening between two men she still cared for.

Sliding into the booth, she leaned her elbows on the table. "Granted, Dax could've picked up the phone to call, too. Or he could've even stopped into the Shack tonight since he was here anyway."

D.J. slowly lowered his menu to the table.

"And," Allaire added, "seeing him unexpectedly like that must've been a jolt."

He merely nodded. But she could tell that, even though there'd been no personal contact tonight, D.J. had scaled an obstacle. Something might've clicked in his brain. Seeing Dax had maybe even caused D.J. to humanize his brother again.

"You know what would be great?" she asked.

"If I forgot everything and just strolled up to Dax and gave him a big old bear hug?"

"Well, I wasn't going to go that far." She reached out to hold his fingers. A thrill whirred up her arm at the warmth of him, at the roughness of his skin, at the size of his capable hands.

She patted him and withdrew, unable to make sense of her reaction. D.J. sank back in his seat, as if disappointed.

Or maybe she was making more out of this than she should.

"It'd be great," she said, "if you could think

about extending the olive branch to Dax by inviting him to the Rib Shack's grand opening. The whole gang is going to be there anyway, right? Grant, Russ, the Cates brothers. What better excuse do you have to see Dax again?"

D.J. paused, then ran a hand over his face and back up through his dark hair. "You're right, Allaire, I know you are. I can't exactly ignore him while I'm in town. It's juvenile."

"*While*…you're in town?" Caught by his terminology, Allaire tried to seem nonchalant, even as her pulse raced. "Are you just passing through, then?"

D.J. reached for the boot-shaped saltshaker, then seemed to reconsider fidgeting. "I haven't decided."

"But you've moved into a cabin at the edge of town, near the Douglas Ranch."

"I'm renting for the time being."

"Oh." She'd assumed he was back for good. But, really, besides the opening of yet another Rib Shack, what reason did he have to stay? An estranged brother? An old friend who had no valid hold on him?

During the uncomfortable silence, he went ahead and grabbed that saltshaker, tracing the tabletop with it. Allaire simply watched him, fixating on the length of his fingers. Out of nowhere, she imagined those fingers brushing her face, exploring it as she, herself, would do to a beloved art subject.

A delicious shiver consumed her and, this time, she actually held on to it, if only to test it out.

And it was good.

"Speaking of family," D.J. said, "how's Arianna?"

Allaire's sister, ten years older and wiser. "She's fine, living in Billings now, working in administration at a radio station."

"Is she still giving the male species hell?"

Allaire couldn't help but smile. D.J. had known every detail of her sister's wild life while Allaire was growing up. She'd confided her concerns about Arianna's restless nature to him religiously, and…wow. She'd missed that. There hadn't been anyone who cared like D.J.—male or female—in her life since he'd left. Not even Tori, who was too new a friend to have the same history.

Heck, what D.J. and Allaire had *now* wasn't even the same; his life was on the climb while hers was on the plunge. She couldn't spill her heart out about the divorce to him; the last thing she wanted was for D.J. to have to choose sides when he should be reconciling with Dax.

By this time, their waitress had greeted them, and they both knew what they wanted to order. D.J. requested the wrangler plate, complete with pan-seared steak, garlic mashed potatoes and ginger-spiced carrots. She went for a simple salad, for which D.J. gave her a bit of guff for ordering, calling it insubstantial.

Ending the silence that followed, she took up where they'd left off. "Arianna got divorce number two, but, this time, she lives out of town so she doesn't have to 'wiggle on the hook of Mom and Dad's displeasure,' as she'd say."

"Poor girl. As if she wasn't having enough of a hard time dealing with baby sister's perfection, and now a pair of divorces?"

"Remember, baby sister has her own disaster to chalk up. Yet I will say this. My parents tend to make excuses for me while they put Arianna through the wringer." Allaire folded her hands in her lap, but her fingers pressed together until they hurt. "Still, no matter what Mom and Dad say, no matter how supportive they've always been, I can see they're put out by my separation from Dax."

D.J. shoved the saltshaker back to its place. "If they've never said anything, how can you be sure?"

"I just know, D.J. Maybe it's in the way they *don't* talk about it."

Since Allaire had always been an over-achiever, she was used to smooth sailing at home. On the other hand, Arianna had cele-brated her mediocrity merely to rankle them, probably thinking she would never match Al-laire, the family's late-born pride and joy, any-way. While Allaire was busy skipping grades, winning class elections and puffing up her col-lege résumé, Arianna was fumbling her way through a divorce. And it wasn't that their par-ents reveled in it; they tried to help any way they could. Still, it was obvious that they weren't surprised Arianna had come to this. It was also clear that they expected Allaire to rise above such failures.

So when Allaire began seriously dating Dax in high school—the golden girl partnered with the popular, charming "bad boy"—her par-ents had ultimately approved, seeing past his fun-loving reputation. He treated Allaire like a princess, assuring her parents that he would be a successful husband and breadwinner on the racing circuit.

Still, all the while, Arianna warned Allaire. "Don't be disappointed when it doesn't work out," Arianna would say while visiting town after having moved so she could get a fresh start elsewhere after her divorce.

When Allaire's marriage had collapsed, her sister's words had haunted her. She believed she'd let everyone down, not just herself.

And for years now, she'd been trying desperately to make up for it.

On the other side of the table, D.J. had been waiting this entire time, simpatico and quiet. Ashamed that she was so transparent, Allaire held back a rush of emotion, trying not to think about what she was feeling. All she wanted to do was get back to her mural, to find herself in a world that she controlled.

"You're too hard on yourself," D.J. said gently. "When are you going to realize that none of us are perfect?"

"The day I lose my standards," she said, attempting a laugh.

But even if D.J. smiled, she knew he wasn't fooled.

Not the man who'd always understood her the best.

* * *

Opening night at the Rib Shack seemed to rush D.J. like a flash flood. Even though he'd been mindful of the upcoming turbulence in the days ahead, he still felt unprepared.

But that was ridiculous, because everything was ready. From the state-of-the-art kitchen to the fully stocked storerooms, from the staff who'd been carefully selected to the far-from-fancy decor, he was ready.

Just as he had been with his other locations.

For tonight, he'd decided to go with a buffet-style presentation so his guests could sample the ribs, side dishes, pies and other down-home fixings at their leisure. In the meantime, the waitstaff circulated trays of Cristal-filled flutes and, of course, bottled beer for the good ol' crowd. The faint scent of barbecue and secret spices hung in the air along with chandeliers bearing dim, flickering lanterns.

But one element was missing. Allaire. He'd seen her right before the doors had opened. She had insisted her mural wasn't ready yet, even though he, in turn, had insisted it was. So, while he saw to the final details of his business, she touched up invisible flaws, then disappeared to change from her grungy work clothes into something suitable for the occasion.

And he was still waiting for her to reappear.

D.J. grabbed a beer from a waiter and lightly thumped him on the back, relating his approval. Across the room by the mural, he found part of the old gang: the dark-haired, dark-eyed Cates brothers. Reticent Mitchell, president and founder of Cates International, and outgoing Marshall, the resort doctor, had already congratulated their pal and were busy entertaining Marshall's steady girlfriend, Mia, by explaining all the painted town images to her.

Then Dax appeared on the other side of the crowded room.

D.J. had to look twice. His brother was wearing a leather jacket as beaten as his composure and, spotting D.J., he hesitated.

Remorse tore down the center of D.J.'s chest, as if separating him in two: the boy who still held a grudge and the man who needed to be big enough to get over it. He decided to honor that side by lifting his hand in a welcoming wave.

Dax looked as if he hardly believed it might be that easy to cross the room and leave behind his own demons. Yet he took his brother up on this olive branch, which had been extended when D.J. had sent an e-mail invitation.

It took Dax a few minutes to thread through the mixed crowd of old friends and D.J.'s business associates, including Lisa and Riley Douglas, the son of the resort's owner. Then, finally reaching D.J., he stood silent for a moment. He was slightly taller than D.J., but right now, he seemed so much less imposing than D.J. remembered.

"Thanks for coming," D.J. said. "I'm glad you're here."

That hadn't been so tough. It must've taken a lot for Dax to show up, so D.J. might as well make it less tense for them both.

Even so, in the back of his mind, he kept seeing the same scene played out: D.J. waking up in a sweat after suffering a nightmare about his mom. D.J. running to his dad's room to reassure himself that he was still there, but finding the bed empty. D.J. knowing exactly where to go next; he would head for the garage, where he would find his father and Dax so immersed in their shared passion for motorcycles—their comfort zone—that they wouldn't ever know that D.J. had been there.

"Glad I came," Dax said, hands on jeaned

hips. He seemed to be making an attempt at being careless, but he came off as slightly defensive instead. "How's Thunder Canyon so far?"

D.J. tried his best to smile. Small talk. But what did he expect—emotional fireworks or even a man-hug from a brother he'd never felt close to?

"So far, so good." D.J. took a gulp of beer, just for something to do. "How's the motorcycle repair business?"

"It keeps me busy."

Silence fell between them again, punctuated only by the festive country music subtly playing over the sound system, leaving room for conversation. If there was any to be had.

Just as D.J. was wondering if their discussion could be any more stilted, he was saved.

"Now the gang's all here," Russ Chilton said, arriving in time to clank D.J.'s beer bottle with his own, then acknowledge Dax with a devilish grin. With his ruffled, dirty-blond hair and hellfire knack for trouble, the rancher had always been a driving force in uncovering a good time or two. "Just had to tell D.J. once again that he knows how to throw a party."

Grant Clifton appeared, tall enough to hover over the group. His designer-suit demeanor served him well as the resort's manager. Stephanie Julen, his ranch forewoman and fiancée, linked arms with him, her youthful, natural beauty balancing Grant's ambitious drive.

"Russ," he said, "tell me you're not over here to bug D.J. about 'giving in to the pressure' and selling out to corporate resort interests again."

"I was kidding the first time." Russ chuckled. "Really, D.J., you're not one of 'them,' even if the resort is squatting here on Thunder Mountain with all the beauty of a pimple."

D.J. couldn't help glancing at Dax, who'd always rebelled against authority. He'd never sold out to anyone, and from the way he was training his gaze on the ground, he agreed with Russ, who had narrowed his brown eyes at something across the room. The group all followed his gaze, finding the object of Russ's attention.

Ah, Melanie McFarlane, a newcomer who'd been causing a ruckus in town. The self-possessed redhead surveyed the room, then spied the gang. She gave a tiny finger wave.

"You *invited* her?" Russ asked D.J.

"I don't…think so." D.J. searched his mind but couldn't recall issuing an invitation. It would've been justified, seeing as Ms. Mc-Farlane, the daughter of East Coast hotel magnates as well as being a manager herself, had come to Thunder Canyon to buy some personal investment property. Actually, she'd had her eye cast toward any ranch she could overhaul, and she'd just purchased the Hopping H. This wasn't sitting well with leave-our-town-alone Russ, in particular.

After helping herself to a flute of champagne from a waiter's tray, she came over to the group, standing opposite Russ and toasting D.J.

"Congratulations, Mr. Traub. I've eaten at the Atlanta Rib Shack and I can't wait to try the one here."

D.J. nodded his thanks, but not before Russ chimed in.

"So you're a regular cowhand now?" he asked.

Ms. McFarlane took the whip-smart remark in stride, but her resulting amusement seemed strained, nonetheless. "I think I prefer the term *trendsetting entrepreneur*."

"You realize," Russ said, "that the Hopping

H. won't be all glamour and fun. I think you don't know what your whims have purchased."

"I think I do," she said. "I think that soon— very, *very* soon—you're going to be eating your opinions like beans at a campfire. But they probably won't go down as easy."

And, with that, Ms. McFarlane tilted her champagne in an emphatic salute, then left the group with a sassy smile.

As she made her way to the buffet table and began piling her plate with food, Russ shook his head. "See what that gold rush encouraged? Attitude. That's what it is. Just plain old irritating, money-sucking attitude…"

Russ continued, but D.J. didn't hear what he was saying. Instead, he'd focused on Stephanie's secretive glance at Grant and how Grant was smiling back down at her as if she were his whole world.

The reality bent into fantasy, one D.J. had never let go of: Allaire by his own side, exchanging the same loving looks with him. *I should've been with you this whole time,* she would say. *I should've known how you felt because I had the same emotions for you, D.J. I just didn't realize it....*

Then he sensed her—Allaire.

She had entered through the boutique hallway door, pausing while absorbing the sparkling crowd, the laughter and good cheer. She'd worn her hair up, as usual, but she was decked out in a dark, tailored, Asian-embroidered long coat that opened at the waist to show off fitted pants. She continued to scan the room with a hint of anxiety about her.

D.J. held his breath, waiting for the moment she'd see him.

Really *see* him.

But her gaze stopped just short of D.J., and his temper rose before he even knew for sure where she was concentrating.

Then he knew.

Dax.

D.J.'s chest seemed to cave in, and it was all he could do not to feel ill at his own grand opening. Was he wrong about how she still felt about his brother?

Was he the world's biggest fool for ever thinking he could compete with Dax?

D.J. barely even noticed when Allaire's gaze continued roaming, then came to rest on him. Had her eyes…lit up? No, he had to be seeing it wrong. The light had to be left over from Dax.

D.J. couldn't kid himself any longer.

As his old friends kept talking, the room seemed to darken around him, even as he fought to be better than this.

Chapter Five

Allaire had come to the Rib Shack opening for one reason only, and when she found him standing across the room, a tiny inner explosion stunned her.

Boom!—it thrust from her very center, her body a vessel that couldn't contain its chemical heat anymore.

She held her breath in the aftermath. This felt good, felt…right.

But, most of all, this felt *crazy*.

As Allaire composed herself, she hoped nobody had seen what had just happened in her own corner of the world. She, a woman who'd never expected a fierce emotion to ever rock her again, felt as if she'd been shredded into a million scraps. But when she and D.J. had connected gazes…

Boom.

Her skin still tingled—sizzling and sensitive. She had been trying to escape D.J. all day by concentrating on her mural. She'd been nervous, thinking about all the people who'd be here tonight, all the old friends and acquaintances who might catch on to how her feelings had changed for her high school pal. And she couldn't allow them to notice, not if she wanted to keep her life safe, neat and perfect.

Gradually, Allaire's surroundings came back into focus. She smoothed her coat, then tuned in to the loud crowd, hoping nobody was talking about the way she'd just about fallen to pieces over one glance from the man of the hour.

But all she heard was laughter swarming in and out of innocuous conversations while country music and the clang of dishes competed in the background.

Then the aroma of D.J.'s barbecue sauce enveloped her, reminding Allaire of how his skin smelled so warm and good when he was near.

As a waitress bustled past, blocking Allaire's view for a split second, she wondered if D.J. might've felt the same combustion when they'd locked glances. But when the waitress cleared away, Allaire saw how his gaze had shuttered, closing her off.

Was it just her then? Was she so desperate for the companionship D.J. had once given her that she was now projecting her wants and needs onto *him?*

Couldn't be. In fact, the more she thought about it, the surer she was. She'd seen something in his eyes a thousand times over. It'd been enough to scare her, because how could she deny what she was feeling for him now?

D.J. had trained his gaze on the ground, then up at her again. In that short space of time, he was already back to being her friend. The guy who'd studied for high school math tests in her family room. The guy who'd sat next to her at assemblies.

His change was so swift, so odd, that she couldn't help thinking that, perhaps, he'd assumed this buddy identity because he knew she wasn't up for anything else.

Allaire finally found her legs and crossed the room, saying hi to the people she knew.

By the time she got to D.J., he had extricated himself from the rest of the gang to intercept her near the food table, where he was already loading up a metal plate. She couldn't help noticing that he wasn't including any meat. Was it for her?

D.J. thought of everything. He'd even allowed her to avoid joining the old gang, no doubt because Dax was there. She'd spotted her ex on the fringes of the group and hadn't been looking forward to greeting him.

Nice, huh? And here she'd been getting after D.J. for doing the same thing. She would make it a point to say hi to her ex soon.

Coming to D.J.'s side, she said, "Looks like you're going to have yet another successful restaurant."

"Time will tell."

As he finished fixing the plate, she tugged at the sleeve of his crisp white shirt. "Sharp, D.J. I guess this is the closest you'll ever come to actual formal wear?"

"And you wondered why I never went to the prom." He smiled but still seemed... Maybe the word was *distracted*. "You know dressing up has never been my thing."

"Too bad, because I think you and a tux would've gotten along just fine."

Whoa—that had come dangerously close to a flirty comment. A wave of warmth roared over her, and she absently flapped a hand in front of her face, stopping only when D.J. noticed.

"Crowded room," she said.

He handed her the plate, and she noted that there was a new meaty-looking entrée off to the side of the hors d'oeuvres. Intrigued, she picked up the sauce-coated strip by its toothpick.

D.J. gestured toward a chafing dish filled with similar pieces. A sign read Vegetarian Barbecue.

"Soy," he said. "*I'm* experimenting. So far, it seems to be going over pretty well, although it'll never come anywhere near the real thing. But a businessman has to keep up with the times."

"A visionary. Thank you, D.J."

She ate the strip, sliding out the toothpick, closing her eyes and making a pleased sound as the sauce bloomed in her mouth.

When she opened her eyes, she found D.J. watching her with what she might've termed great interest. The part of her that she didn't know very well reveled in his gaze, too. It goaded Allaire to take her time in chewing. In smiling at him with approval and contentment.

But when a man in a pinstripe suit sauntered by and greeted D.J., Allaire caught herself and fixed her gaze on her plate.

Boy, that'd been strange. It wasn't like her to be recreating a scene from *Tom Jones* in public.

And with D.J., of all people.

As he traded greetings with the pin-striped guest, Allaire recovered enough to notice that D.J.'s skin had reddened, two bright spots on his cheeks announcing either embarrassment or…

Nope, she wasn't going to think of what else it could be.

Meanwhile, she concentrated on the rib sauce serenading her taste buds. Wow. She grabbed a few more strips from the chafing dish.

Soon, Pinstripes ended the greeting, waving to someone else across the festivities. D.J. shrugged and faced Allaire again, scanning her replenished plate.

"You've won me over," she said.

"It's about time."

He cleared his throat, as if covering what he'd just said, then walked over to a waiter carrying champagne. While Allaire tried to get a bead on what was going on between them, he brought back a flute for her.

She accepted the glass and sent a pointed look toward Russ and Grant's group. Dax was still planted firmly on the edges, where he liked it best. "I saw that you and your brother were actually in the same corner of the room. Good for you."

Suddenly, D.J. seemed to ice over.

Had getting back into contact with Dax been even harder than she'd thought for D.J.?

"Did it go badly?" she asked.

"It was all right. We're fine."

A slew of unidentifiable emotions swirled in his eyes—eyes that always made her think of the good earth. Yet there seemed to be so much buried inside of him, too, and Allaire only wished he would dig some more of it up to share with her.

But, for the time being, it was enough to get the brothers within talking range of each other.

Taking a sip of the champagne, she wandered toward a jukebox in the corner. She could feel the heat of D.J. following her, could hear people congratulating and complimenting him.

Pride slid over her heart, enclosing it as she leaned against a planked wall near the music machine. He stood near her, beer in hand, while she set her flute and plate on the slim shelf running the length of the wall.

She nibbled on the exquisite corn bread, then said, "Look at you. The new D.J.—restaurateur and cover boy for *BusinessWeek Magazine*. I feel like I barely know this guy."

"Come on, Allaire."

"No, really. Does this D.J. still like comic books and model planes?"

He grinned. "You mean, am I still a geek?"

Taken aback, she smacked him lightly. "Need I remind you that I sat in your room when we were freshmen and read comics right along with you?"

"That's because I kept mentioning that you resembled a certain caped girl of steel, and you liked that. You said you 'related.'"

And she had: blond hair, blue eyes and a duty to live up to high responsibility. Yup, Allaire had definitely related, suspecting all along that she wasn't even close to being as super as she should be.

"Okay, okay," she said. "I also helped you with your model planes, so I guess I'm a geek, too. Do you still fiddle around with all that stuff?"

"I gave those and the comics away when I went to college. Still, I suppose I never really got out of the habit of putting planes together."

"What do you mean?"

D.J. angled his beer bottle as he spread out his hands. "I mess around with sailplanes now. In fact, I had my newest one shipped over here."

Allaire laughed, delighted that the scale-model D.J. had graduated to bigger versions of the same thing. "What exactly is a sailplane? I can take a fair guess, but…"

"Mine is a motorless, enclosed, fiberglass resin plane."

"Motorless. So…these aren't little itty-bitty items you stick on a shelf."

"No, they can fly. With me in them."

Without knowing it, Allaire held a hand to her chest. She couldn't count how many times she'd wanted to soar like D.J. obviously did on a regular basis.

"How do you fly the things if they don't have a motor?" she asked.

"I use an aero tow." D.J.'s enthusiasm was obvious—his gaze had gone bright, his words animated. "I'll show you sometime, but only after the plane is in good enough shape. The engineer I work with was at the portable hangar near my cabin tinkering with her just this afternoon."

"I'd like to take a peek at it, all right." Allaire enjoyed seeing D.J. happy and carefree like this. It was a nice change. "I'd like it a lot."

The moment lifted, swelling to fill the space that had fallen between them earlier. Then Marshall Cates called for D.J. to join him while he headed toward the rest of their old friends.

D.J. motioned that he'd be over soon. Unfortunately, the interruption popped their moment right open, putting Allaire and D.J. back where they'd started.

D.J. seemed to recognize that. He shoved a hand into his pocket. "And what about you? Any new hobbies besides what I already know about? Any new passions?"

A spike of awareness made her reach for the champagne. Passions. Yes, she'd developed one of those real recently, but telling him about the way she'd been reacting to him wasn't an option.

But what about hobbies?

She sifted through her mind for something fresh to offer him. But, sadly, nothing else had altered within her. Well, that is unless you counted the frustration and disappointment that had been introduced over the years. Like her art, it seemed as if she would always be a work in progress.

"You might've gone from models to the real thing, but not me." She paused, at a loss, then remembered something small but worth mentioning. "I've furthered my art research, I guess. There's that."

If a person were to judge by D.J.'s reaction, they'd think Allaire had just told him she'd scaled Mount Everest.

"No surprise there," he said. "You were never content with seeing paintings in library books, so you used to plan trips based on how good the museums would be in each city."

She sipped her drink. D.J. was clearly under the false impression that she'd traveled out of Thunder Canyon on her own. That she'd seen all those highlighted areas on the world map she'd kept pinned to her bedroom wall.

"D.J., I still just look at those library books."

Getting the message, he made as if to give her a sympathetic pat, but it never quite reached her arm. "You've got your whole life ahead of you to see all you want."

That's what she'd told herself last year, and the year before, yet she'd never seemed to have enough extra money to spend on a summer trip. Not when she invested so much of her paychecks in art supplies for both her classroom and her own apartment's mini-studio.

She tried to inject some optimism into the conversation. Bringing D.J. down to her level wasn't pleasant at all.

"I learned to play the piano," she said, "and I have an electronic keyboard that I poke around on when I'm trying to feel my way through an art piece that's giving me a hard time. Walking also helps me think, too. I've been meaning to start hiking more."

"Hiking." She could tell that D.J. was doing his best to make her feel better. "Now, I didn't get to do *that* much in Atlanta, but here I am, in one of the most gorgeous areas of the U.S., so…"

"So maybe we can take one soon. Before it starts raining all the time."

"And before the first snow."

There it was again, a kind of bubble around them, keeping everyone at bay while they enjoyed each other's company. She'd thought the ability to forget about the outside world had disappeared with the onset of adulthood.

Or did it only happen with D.J.?

For the next half hour, people kept passing by and saying hello, then leaving when they saw how D.J. and Allaire were too into their conversation to devote much attention to anyone else. They talked about the best areas to hike around Thunder Canyon, talked about all the places they'd love to go. They even started to joke about the ultimate American road trip.

Until someone broke their bubble.

"To D.J.'s Rib Shack!" said a stocky blond man, chiming in to thump D.J. on the arm.

Both Allaire and D.J. blinked at the high school acquaintance, Tommy Churchill. He'd just gotten off a plane from Wyoming this morning, returning home to work as a snow sports instructor at the resort.

Although Allaire could tell D.J. didn't love being interrupted, he politely accepted Tommy's kudos, also thanking him for attending.

After the other man finished telling D.J. how

great it was to be back in Thunder Canyon, he clumsily raised his beer bottle toward Allaire.

"Allaire Buckman," he said. "How're you doing?"

"Traub. I go by Traub." She didn't think anything of correcting Tommy since she'd lived with the last name for years. She hadn't even changed it after the divorce since that's who she'd become, really. That's how everyone knew her.

Out of the corner of her eye, she noticed that D.J. had gone stiff again. Was it because Dax had crept into the discussion?

Tommy jokingly hit himself upside the head. "Sorry, sorry. I just remember things like they were way back when. I forgot you married Dax. How's the king of motor racing?"

Automatically, her damage-control function kicked in. *Let Tommy know you tried. Let him know that you're fine and that the divorce didn't ruin your life....*

But before she could start explaining, D.J. backed out of the discussion, seeming ill at ease. Then he was gone, swallowed by the crowd.

D.J. deposited his bottle at a table by the door, then walked out into the chilly night.

Who cared if he didn't have a coat? His skin was already numb.

He just needed air, needed…

Crap, what *did* he need?

He knew the answer, and she was still inside, chatting with Tommy Churchill about her marriage to Dax.

He'd known that coming back to Thunder Canyon guaranteed an avalanche of reminders. Hell, he'd been all too willing to endure them, too.

So why was he losing his determination to withstand all the talk now?

As D.J. braced himself against the slap of cold, he took a right, wandering along the outside of the main lodge's boutique hallway, its lights cutting the night. Meanwhile, he calmed himself, promising he'd go back in after a few head-clearing minutes.

Good. The chill flowing through his lungs was working enough for him to realize that, in the big picture, he merely needed more time to adjust to the way life was now. And adjust he would. After all, look at tonight. He'd made a decent start with Dax….

Dax. King of motor racing. King of everything.

Images assaulted D.J.: his dad and Dax laughing with each other at a private joke only the two of them understood while they all attempted a "family" dinner at the table. Allaire reclining against the school's brick wall as Dax leaned over, resting his arm over her head as he kissed her.

A red filter covered D.J.'s memories. He'd spent all this time taming his anger. But, now, in the town where that rage had been born, how could D.J. avoid repressing his bitterness about Dax anymore?

D.J. fisted his hands. It'd been one thing to forget his pain while he was on the other side of the country, but it was another to think he wouldn't be affected right here, right now, when it all seemed like yesterday. A tightness banded within his chest, stretching like a sling ready to spear his self-control into the air.

My weakness put me in this position. Nothing else.

His attempt to fight off the resentment wasn't working; it only made the sling go tighter.

I *allowed Dax to "steal" Allaire from me.*

Tighter still.

And I'm *allowing Dax to puppet me around*

right now, working my strings without even knowing it.

And tighter....

Even though D.J. wished it could be different, the anger felt good. Rage had been his driving force all these years. It'd given him purpose when the death of his mom had seemed to take every bit of it away. It'd made him *feel,* at the very least, while he'd numbly watched Dax charm Allaire, then marry her.

Even now, as D.J. fought to quell his emotions, a part of him held desperately to the rancor, maybe even out of the fear that he'd have nothing left if he let it die—

"You left your own party," said a voice from behind him.

D.J. would know that voice anywhere, even if he hadn't heard much of it in a long time.

Dax.

The veins in D.J.'s forehead strained. This was probably the worst timing in recorded history.

"I needed a break from all the gabbing," he said. "I'll be back soon."

"All right." Pause. "I thought I'd check in with you. That's all I wanted."

The repressed part of D.J.—the part waiting

for that sling to let fly like he was an arrow on fire—had an answer for Dax's "checking in."

Well, you've fulfilled all the big-brother requirements for the year. Now go away.

But all the better-intentioned D.J. could do was offer something like a grunt in answer.

Unfortunately, a vague sound wasn't good enough for Dax. He kept standing there, breathing until D.J. wanted to clap his hand over his sibling's mouth because it irked him so much.

Couldn't Dax read a room? Or was he too stubborn to leave D.J. to collect himself?

"You know," Dax said, "I was surprised you came back home after all this time."

In the distance, a wolf howled. The sound struck an animalistic chord in D.J.

He only wanted to be left alone, but his brother wouldn't even give him that.

D.J. turned around, almost afraid of what seeing Dax would do to his temper. But what he witnessed didn't add heat to his emotions as much as put them on a still-flaming side burner.

The moonlight enfolded his brother as if attracted to him, but the illumination wasn't working its usual magic on the king of Thunder Canyon High. No, instead, the light only served to emphasize what had happened to Dax in the interim, how his ego had clearly been chipped in some way.

D.J. realized something—if he kept *himself* mired in this resentment, maybe he was in for a similar fate. It'd be a damned shame, too, seeing as he'd gained so much in Atlanta. Self-assurance, riches…

All of it gone, just like Dax's lost sheen.

But everyone shaped themselves into what they became, wasn't that the truth? D.J. had been afraid to be the "shadow son," the lesser of two Traub boys, but he'd made his fears a reality. He'd refused to stand up for what he had wanted, with their dad and then with Allaire. He'd been so afraid that Dax was the better man that D.J., himself, had made that a certainty.

And tonight, when Allaire had entered the room and looked at Dax first, that fear of being nothing next to his brother had returned to D.J. full force.

But now, looking at Dax and seeing that he'd fallen from his arrogant pedestal, D.J. felt his expression turn sympathetic, his fury lacking fire, even though it still seethed.

Dax seemed to catch on to D.J.'s altered mood—which he would probably translate as pity. And Dax had never done pity.

He assumed that cock-of-the-walk lift of the head.

"Dax…" D.J. started.

"I also never thought you'd sell out, D.J." He nodded to the Rib Shack. He was talking about the resort, the corporate takeover of Thunder Canyon. "Dad taught us better than that."

Dad didn't care to teach me much of anything, D.J. wanted to say. But he refrained. It would hurt too damned much to admit out loud.

Besides, he wasn't going to play his brother's game. Dax was suddenly bringing up this subject because he was getting defensive, that's all. D.J. had endured years of his older brother taunting him into fights just so Dax could assert his dominance, or at least that's what D.J. had thought. Truth be told, D.J. had itched for every showdown; he'd been willing to rumble just because Father had loved Dax best.

But D.J. had to be better than this.

Better than Dax.

The thought added fuel to D.J.'s rage again. Competition, sibling rivalry. Allaire…

"Is this the conversation you want to be having with me?" D.J. asked. "Is this how we should start out with each other?"

For a moment, D.J. saw the naked answer on his sibling's face. No, Dax didn't want it to be this way, but he still had pride. It was as if he were clinging to what was left of it just as tenaciously as D.J. held to his own resentment.

What was eating away at his brother? Why was he acting like this when it was obvious that D.J. was on edge?

Dax stepped nearer, lowering his voice. "You're right. Maybe we should go back inside, where I can get a beer and you can keep making eyes at Allaire."

D.J.'s brain wasn't really processing what his brother had just said. But his body had responded, all right. It tensed up, from bunched fists to readied stance.

"Care to repeat that?"

Don't fall for this, D.J. Walk away. That's all you have to do....

"Don't play it innocent." Dax laughed, but it sounded self-directed. "You're all over Allaire like a bad suit."

The insinuation that D.J. wasn't fit for the

woman of his dreams finally got him. Deep down, he'd been waiting for Dax to cross a line.

Maybe he'd also been waiting for someone to voice his own self-doubts, and Dax had been the unfortunate one to do it.

Before D.J. could stop himself, he bolted over to his brother and held up an index finger to make a point. He must've instinctively recalled how much Dax hated the pointing finger and how it'd always goaded him when the brothers sparred.

"You were the only one good enough for her, is that it, Dax? Even though you could've had your pick of any girl, you decided on Allaire, and even though..."

"Even though what, D.J.?" Dax didn't back off. "Say it. I'm sick of being blamed for the whole world's problems, so why don't you just lay it out? Tell me how terrible I was for *stealing* Allaire from you."

Had Dax *known* how D.J. felt about Allaire? And had he swooped in to take her away in spite of how his own younger brother had felt?

D.J.'s blood boiled to the point where he could barely contain himself.

"Ah, got it," Dax said, his mood getting even surlier. Maybe he didn't like that D.J. hadn't punched him yet. "You're going to play it honorable. That's how it always was—Sir D.J., willing to suffer nobly in his pain. Silent D.J., who'd rather leave a situation than stay and fight for what he wanted."

A flare shot through D.J., and he barely refrained from lashing out. But it was hard, and he didn't know how long he could stand here and take this.

"I left Thunder Canyon because—"

"You *left*," Dax said, "and Dad fell to pieces."

A low humming droned in D.J.'s head. "What're you talking about?"

Dax's words were clenched. "He missed you. Every time you two talked on the phone, he'd go into a funk. He said he regretted not paying more attention to you when we were young, that he'd driven you away. I always told him he was wrong, but he didn't want to hear it."

"Are..." D.J. began to tremble at the restraint. "Are you accusing me of being the reason Dad's heart gave out?"

When Dax took too long to answer, D.J.'s vision roared to red, his fist flying out to connect with his brother's jaw.

Dax stumbled back, holding his hand to his

face and smiling. But it was a smile that held all kinds of self-hatred.

D.J.'s knuckles stung as he stood there, stunned at what he'd just done.

But when his older sibling dove at him, he was ready. He'd been primed for a fight for years now. With every punch to the gut, every grunt and shove, he played out his rage. And when he took each of Dax's punches, he accepted the breathless anguish as punishment.

The brothers fell to the ground, a mass of knuckles and curses as they worked out their problems in the only way they knew how: physically.

Yet, soon, their knocks lost force. Oxygen felt heavy and sharp in D.J.'s lungs, and he realized that Dax was taking longer to return the punches, just as D.J. was getting slower to deliver them.

"Why…" Dax panted, "didn't you…ever… tell me how you…felt about her?"

Slam went his fist into D.J.'s stomach.

D.J. *oof*ed, taking the brunt of it. Then he swiftly rolled to a dominant position, bracing the blade of his arm against Dax's collarbone.

"You…wouldn't have…listened…anyway…"

he managed, right before Dax shoved at D.J., levering him off.

Then Dax pushed D.J. farther backward and got to his knees, lifting his fists, ready for more.

"Maybe…" he said, "I *would've*…listened."

The two of them sat there, gasping for air, facing off.

Then, as if in agreement, they fell away from each other, coming to lean their backs against the lodge. D.J. realized just how cold it was out there as the night stung his skin and lungs.

Their words even looked like smoke from a burned-out fire.

"Why didn't…you ever…tell me what you…" Dax's words trailed off. His hair was even more ruffled, his face cut.

D.J. touched a spot near his eye. His fingers came away with blood, and the sight of red there instead of over his gaze made him realize that he'd spent his ill will.

For now, at least.

"That I…what?" D.J. asked, still hedging because he didn't want to say her name.

Allaire.

Yup, D.J. had been physically bruised, but a

mental thrashing would be far worse, so he still had to play it safe by refusing to spill his guts.

Dax held his jaw. "You know what I'm talking about, dumb-ass. I wish you would've said something early on. Why didn't you?"

D.J. found a leaf and brushed his wet hand over it. "It wouldn't have mattered."

Smoke continued to steam the air as Dax huffed, recovering. Then, "You know how it felt to see my own brother looking at Allaire like you did at my wedding reception?"

D.J. froze. Good God.

"Yeah," Dax added, "I saw that torn expression on your face when we were doing that champagne toast after the ceremony. Son of a bitch, what was I supposed to do when all of your dedication and devotion to her suddenly made sense? I loved Allaire, you know, even though things fell apart. I never thought that would happen."

D.J. closed his eyes, unbearable agony thrusting up until it ripped at the inside of his throat.

"I can't believe you never told her," Dax said wearily. "If you felt so damned strongly, I can't believe you didn't ever say anything."

D.J. hesitated, but the pressure to explain

was too much. "I can't believe I kept my silence, either. I've beaten myself up about it for years, but you were…you *are* my brother. What kind of man steals a sibling's woman away like that?"

The rest went unsaid. Neither of them had to mention that maybe a man might have no idea that his own younger brother loved that same woman, so he'd gone ahead and "stolen" her. Or maybe there was simply no chance for any kind of understanding between those brothers, and whatever they did to each other wouldn't matter anyway.

As their breathing eventually smoothed out, D.J. realized that it didn't feel so terrible to be sitting next to Dax. They'd thumped all the tension out of each other for the time being.

And that's how Allaire found them: bloody, bruised and smack-dab at halftime in a conversation about her.

Chapter Six

When Allaire saw the brothers slumped against the outside wall, she darted over, panicking at the sight of blood on D.J.'s face.

Not Dax's face, but D.J.'s.

"What the devil is going on?" she asked.

Neither man said a word. They merely leveled taut looks at one another. Then, as Allaire brushed D.J.'s hair away from his forehead so she could get a better assessment of his wounds, Dax watched.

She concentrated on the blood, the cuts, the swelling. "Are you both eleven years old or something? I swear, when Grant said he saw you two going outside within minutes of each other, I got curious. But I didn't expect this."

Sending an exasperated glance to Dax in particular—he'd been in his share of fights growing up—she got ready to unleash another comment. But then she caught the look on his face.

It was as if he were resigned in some way. As if he were accepting a truth that was beyond her.

Then a lightbulb went on inside her head. Here she was fussing over D.J., touching him gently while Dax sat there unattended.

Allaire glanced back at D.J., finding that his gaze had gone soft while her fingers cupped his cheek.

Slowly, she backed away from him. She'd run to D.J. first and not the man she'd once been in love with. What did that mean?

She reminded herself of her place. Best friend. *Best. Friend.*

"Fighting," she said, putting all her emotion into what they'd done instead of what she was feeling. "Instead of talking to each other like grown-ups, you were slugging it out. Very mature, you two."

Again, silence from the Traub brothers. If

Allaire didn't know better, she would even say that they were engaged in a strange alliance to keep quiet. It was a tenuous one, at best, but it seemed to be there all the same.

"Okay then." She was Miss All-Business now, leaning toward Dax to check out his injuries in the dim lighting provided by the lodge and the moon. In fact, she sort of made a point of showing that she intended to give equal attention to both men. "Will you at least tell me what you two were trading punches about?"

She reached out to test a cut swelling near Dax's chin. He flinched away, holding up a hand to make sure she didn't connect.

Strangely enough, she only felt annoyed. One would think his rejection would've conjured a stronger emotion in her. But maybe their marriage had spent so much time in free-fall that there was no feeling left after the final crash.

Dax spoke, his hand still up. "Would you believe it if I told you we both got tangled up with a wayward moose?"

D.J. laughed quietly, a hard sound.

"Oh, ha-ha. How droll you can be." Allaire stood away from them, hands on her hips. "I'm supposed to let this go by without comment, I suppose. I know it's not for me to be sticking my nose into things, but I'm not just going to stand by while this nonsense happens. Maybe you should go back to avoiding each other."

As they remained mum, her anger boiled. Darn it all, she was sick of being left in the dark with them.

D.J. stirred, but it was only to dab at his injured lip and lift his thumb to see the blood. Dax casually came to a stand, acting as if fighting had been on his to-do list and he'd just now checked it off.

"Where're you going?" she asked.

"Home, where it's warm."

Now that he mentioned it, Allaire realized she was freezing out here. Her cheeks felt as if they'd suffered a good cuffing, and the air had crept through her long coat without her even having known it. She'd been too ticked off to notice.

"I'm sure there's a first aid kit inside the Shack," she said. "I'll—"

"Forget it." Dax sauntered past her, heading in the direction of the parking lot. He looked like he was carrying the weight of the world on his shoulders. "I'm done for the night."

"I guess you are." Allaire breathed on her hands and rubbed them briskly.

"Listen, I don't need it from you, too, Allaire."

Before she could ask what "it" was, Dax paused and glanced at D.J., who was still sitting against the wall. He'd draped an arm over one bent knee as he narrowly watched his brother.

Dax shook his head and tugged a hand through his hair, a habit D.J. shared when he was frustrated. "D.J., just…forget what I said about Dad, all right? It wasn't altogether true. Not the part that made you think you were responsible for his death, anyway."

He started walking away but then seemed to think better of it. Exhaling, he paused, then added, "He did miss you, though."

D.J. stared straight ahead, unreadable.

That must have gotten to Dax because, with a muttered curse, he headed back toward his younger brother. Allaire went on guard until she realized that Dax wasn't *stalking* toward D.J. She'd even go so far as to say that his movements were rather reluctant.

What Dax uttered next was barely audible, but when he glanced back at her before whispering to D.J., she frowned.

"Just open your eyes and do what you need to *now,* you brick-head."

Then he left D.J. and Allaire to stare at his retreating back.

Music from inside the Shack muffled its way into the night. What could she say to fill the hole Dax had just left?

And…what should D.J. open his eyes to?

As D.J. lowered his gaze, Allaire had a bad feeling she might understand everything: what they'd been fighting about in addition to their dad, why stubborn, proud Dax might have stormed off.

Had he instructed his younger brother to recognize Allaire's immediate concern for D.J. after she'd seen the blood? Was he trying to point out that Allaire had acted like a woman who felt more for D.J. than just friendship?

Or had their disagreement centered only around their dad, and she was imagining the rest?

She didn't think so. Dax had given her quite the pointed look before commenting to D.J.

God, why hadn't she used her head before rushing to fuss over D.J. first?

Her conscience told her loud and clear: *your feelings for D.J. aren't what you always as-*

sumed they were, Allaire. You've developed a real thing for him....

She couldn't lie to herself any longer. Even Dax had noticed the truth tonight. But... Good heavens, this was D.J.

And all the baggage that came with discovering her new feelings for him.

As the night sifted around them, she felt his gaze on her. She met his eyes, recognizing his anxiety as her own. Being called out by Dax was a bigger injury than any punch could inflict, but at least *he* was holding up under it.

Clearly, D.J. was waiting for her to either deny the truth about what was happening to them or embrace it.

As Allaire tried to decide what she should do, her body shot sparks against her skin. The white flares burned through her flesh, branding her.

Open your *eyes, Allaire. And your mouth.*

But she couldn't say a word, because that would force her to destroy what was safe about D.J. She couldn't allow anything beyond a friendship, because failing in another more intimate relationship would beat her down for good.

Arianna would've seconded that opinion.

"You're just gonna get decimated in the end," her sister would say, speaking from awful experience.

However, the moment for either her or D.J. to take up the truth and run with it had passed. And, naturally, D.J. was the one who made her feel better about losing the opportunity.

"I guess we should go back inside then."

But when he started to get to his feet, he groaned. Allaire rushed forward out of instinctive worry for him.

"You okay?" She guided him back down to the ground.

"Maybe I'll wait for my bruises to stop screaming."

"Then you'll be out here all night." She ached to touch his face again, but she refrained, knowing what a touch might unleash in this fragile moment. "You're not going anywhere looking like that moose picked a fight with you."

"Then what do you suggest?"

Allaire glanced around, finding an iron bird fountain yards away. She rushed to it, scooping out water with one palm, then came back.

"That's going to freeze my face off," he grumbled.

His voice was too deep. It was also ragged enough to indicate he was wary of her touch, especially after what his brother had said.

"Then brace yourself." She dipped her fingers into the cold water and bent to him.

D.J. took it like the man he was, clenching his jaw as she wiped the blood away from his cuts. When he shivered, she couldn't blame him.

But she wondered… Was he reacting to the water or…her?

At the latter possibility, warmth suffused her core, turning to a streak of hot desire. Her belly awakened with a yearning that dripped downward.

She tried to hold back, but it was too much. Touching D.J., knowing that maybe this man who'd cared so much for her in his youth had developed more than platonic feelings now. She'd missed being appreciated, missed the stimulation of being attracted to someone, even though she'd lived just fine without all that.

After nursing D.J.'s other wounds—the shiner, the various facial cuts—she traced her thumb over the last one: the mild slice near his mouth. Unable to help herself, she stroked the swollenness, realizing how full his bottom lip was, how soft.

Why hadn't she ever noticed?

"Allaire," he whispered, sending a stream of voltage through her.

She glanced up. His gaze was filled with a longing so intense that her entire being live-wired, trembling from the increasing vibrations.

Then, before she realized what was happening, he slid his hand to the back of her head, drawing her down to meet his lips.

The heat of his skin shocked her, then scratched her face with its emerging stubble. But she didn't mind that—no, she was too overwhelmed by his warm lips, still wet from the water. The moisture made their kiss fluid, as easy as a stroke of paint over canvas.

Utterly captured, her mind emptied of everything except for pastel shades of color, swirls of pink and blue, like a cloud-stretched sky at dawn. She pressed against D.J., soaring, sipping at him as he buried his fingers in her hair and spread his other hand over the small of her back, urging her even tighter against him.

So *this* was what it was like to kiss the guy who used to be her best friend....

Her breasts flattened against his hard chest. Muscular, she thought, strong. A man. D.J. had become such a man.

A flame fanned out in her chest, thawing her fears as passion soaked her. She opened her mouth more, encouraging him to do the same. She stroked his tongue with hers, establishing a sultry rhythm, devouring him with gluttonous ecstasy.

He made a sound low in his throat, a primal call that made her innocent mental pictures of clouds and sky melt crimson with shuddering need. She slid her hand to the back of his head, where she clutched his hair, almost pulling at it as she kept deepening the kiss.

Long, slow draws…a revelation…

He disengaged, then brushed his mouth against hers again. Her hair had come undone, tumbling down her back as she splayed across his lap. Both of them breathed heavily as he kept nipping at her lips.

"You don't know…" he whispered between sweet kisses, "how many times I've…"

"Shh, D.J." She just wanted him to keep doing what he'd been doing—pummeling her with sensation.

But this break had also tinted her mind with

reality, bringing blackness to the colors of their kisses.

There she goes, trying to notch another Traub into her lipstick case....

She didn't get it right the first time. Does she think she's going to be any more successful with D.J.?

Before his lips could make her forget the *real* truth—that Allaire had no business getting close to him—she forced herself to sit up, to push away.

To come to her senses.

D.J.'s hands remained up, suddenly emptied.

"Wow," she said, not knowing what else to offer. She didn't want him to feel bad about what had just happened. She merely wouldn't let it happen again.

"Yeah…wow," he said.

As she straightened her coat and got to her knees, her buzz gradually wore off, leaving her freezing again. Her mind began to function. How was she going to explain the dirt on her pants to everyone? Wouldn't the party guests think something was up if she and D.J. appeared together after a lengthy absence?

Not that they would care after seeing D.J.'s

injuries, but she'd been trained to be neurotic. Logic didn't matter.

Her heart was rattling, like an engine that wouldn't stop correctly after it'd been shut off. Her breath came in shallow chops. Even her head was still swimming.

She wanted…

No. She wouldn't let herself have him because he was just going to disappear anyway once love showed its true colors.

When she caught sight of D.J.'s devastated expression, she stood, finding her throat was too choked to let any words past it.

And, before she could go back to his kisses, she left, walking, then running to the parking lot.

Stunned, D.J. watched her go, not knowing what the hell to do. Not knowing if she would tolerate him following her.

Had he messed up?

Every cell of him was still on fire, blasting like a furnace stoked by a tiny bit of the fuel it required to run properly.

Everything about him was running right, but clearly he *had* done wrong.

Had he misread her?

He replayed the kiss, how she'd been so close to him, her perfume like a sachet hidden beneath a nighttime pillow. How she'd run her thumb over his mouth, as if inviting him. How he'd taken that invitation and she'd responded.

Hell, yeah, she'd definitely responded.

D.J. closed his eyes, his head thudding back against the wall. He'd never imagined a kiss so powerful. And it had merely been that— a kiss. He couldn't even picture what more would do to him.

Absently, he touched his mouth, which was still swollen from her kisses. A brighter man would've said that Dax's punches had actually done the trick, but D.J. knew that Allaire had been the one to bring out the joy, the pain, of feeling. Dax hadn't...

Damn it, Dax.

D.J. allowed his hand to fall away from his lips.

Back in the real world.

He stood, then headed toward the Rib Shack entrance, every step pounding memory into his brain, mimicking the punches he and Dax had traded.

Just open your eyes and do what you need to now, *you brick-head.*

If Allaire hadn't returned D.J.'s kisses with such passion, he might not have believed Dax. How had his estranged brother known what Allaire was feeling even before D.J. himself had been certain?

Dax's blunt comment had given D.J. the bravery to finally make a move, and it had paid off. In spades. Yet…

Yet Allaire had run away from him in the end. She felt something for D.J. that went beyond friendship—he knew that without a doubt—but she wasn't accepting it.

And how could she, with Dax and the remains of their marriage still between them?

Inhaling, he prepared to hide his injuries and re-enter his party. At the same time, he had no clue as to what would—or *should*—happen next.

In the aftermath, Allaire decided to take a few days to get her head together as far as D.J. was concerned.

It wasn't that she was hesitant to see him again. Heck, no. All she wanted to do was get herself back to him and take up where they'd left off. She wanted to explore more, go deeper into him.

And that's *exactly* why she was playing hermit, putting off returning the voice mail he'd left yesterday.

She was surreptitiously staring at her cell phone screen again when Tori wandered into Allaire's classroom and caught her.

"Just call already," the English teacher whispered.

Allaire shot her friend the major look of death, then jerked her head to the studio portion of the classroom, where a group of students was adding final touches to the projects that were due tomorrow. Having come after school, they were laboring diligently, with only the occasional spurt of gossip.

Tori slid her plan book onto a table desk opposite Allaire. They'd decided to synchronize a few lessons so their common students could meld literature themes from Tori's class and use them for artistic inspiration in Allaire's.

"What?" Tori whispered again. Then she used her fingers to punctuate her next words. "Are. We. Going. To. Talk. In. Code?"

Allaire lowered her voice and used her hands, too, her back to her students. "Not. A. Bad. Idea."

Smiling, Tori seized Allaire's phone, then set

it aside. "You're torturing yourself with this." Her whisper fell to an even softer level. "It was only a kiss."

Only a kiss. Sure. And Michelangelo's *David* was *only* a statue.

Tori caught Allaire's shake of the head.

"Was it actually…more?" her friend asked.

"No. No-o-o-o." Allaire glanced behind her to find some of the kids talking and giggling as they sculpted. She focused back on Tori. "A kiss was enough. Believe me."

Enough to have her world spinning even three days later.

"I still don't get why you aren't going for it." Tori sighed, then whispered with more enthusiasm. "D.J.'s hot in that quiet-guy way. Then again, a man doesn't have to say much to pull *my* trigger."

"Too much information."

Tori just smiled. "So. When are you going back to the Rib Shack to touch up your mural? You can just talk to him then and not bother with a call."

Allaire doodled in her plan book. "I, ah, went back last night after hours."

Tori gave her a do-not-hold-out-on-me look.

"I used the set of keys D.J. gave me." Allaire

stopped scribbling, realizing that her doodle was turning out an awful lot like a soft, sexy mouth. *D.J.*'s mouth. "I haven't given them back yet."

"Issues," Tori said softly.

"Like you don't have them, too." But if Allaire continued obsessing about D.J. and why she should or shouldn't see him, she'd definitely be a candidate for the trash heap soon.

She'd tried hard to lose herself in work, as usual. But she kept remembering how D.J. had looked upon seeing her Paris painting during Open-School Night, and she found herself concentrating more on him than on furthering her progress on the piece itself. She'd even attempted to start a new project, a wire sculpture, but what she'd intended to shape into an abstract statement on the differences in world cultures had turned into more of an homage to silly hearts. It was embarrassing to have her serious intentions reduce themselves to something a freshman would be etching into a tree trunk.

"I don't understand," Tori whispered, "why you mess around with the mural if you've already decided that it's the best work you've ever done."

"Because it can be better."

"Allaire, you're gonna run yourself ragged thinking your best is never good enough."

"And you're gonna fit right into the group who goes to The Hitching Post to gossip if you don't stop with the social observations."

Tori raised her hands—*Bring it on*—hardly realizing that the subject was much closer to Allaire's heart than she ever let on. The other day during her lunch break, Allaire had stopped in at The Hitching Post, which was a couple doors down from the dinner theater. She'd just wanted to drop off a replacement for a painted tree that a cast member had broken, then take out a salad. But she'd gotten more.

As she'd sat at the bar, under the notorious portrait of *The Shady Lady,* she'd caught patches of conversation from a far table. The occupants, who had recently started to use the establishment for book club meetings, judging from the five copies of *The Poisonwood Bible* on the table, must not have realized that Allaire's hearing worked just fine.

"…hear about all the time she spent on that mural she painted up at the resort for D.J.?" one of them said. "Talk about an excuse for her to get close enough to pounce."

Red-faced at the proof that her fears about town gossip had become a reality, Allaire had blocked out the rest of it, too embarrassed about what the group might have heard about her and D.J. and how far they were going to take their idle talk. She couldn't control what other people said, but Allaire could darn well control what she *did* and, hence, cut off any more gossip.

And that had to include staying away from D.J.

Having nothing more to say to Tori on the subject of kisses, Allaire started lesson planning, and her friend fell into step. They spent a half hour going over ideas before the other teacher stood and prepared to go.

Allaire gathered her materials, too. "I guess I should drop by the dinner theater before the show starts to see if that tree's holding up."

"Honey, leave those sets alone. You're done with them. Done!"

So much for whispering. The students took one look at their teachers and began talking themselves, gossiping about the approaching homecoming dance and who was going to take whom.

Tori winked at Allaire, then said goodbye to the kids as she strolled out of the room.

Allaire suspected it might be time to leave soon since the teens didn't seem so keen to work on their projects anymore. She began to arrange the art books that the kids had been referencing earlier.

"So," she said, "are you ar-teests planning on being locked in after I leave in fifteen, or are you wrapping it up?"

That got them hustling to finish. Still, the small crowd couldn't help more homecoming chatter, and Allaire even enjoyed their exuberance, wondering why their brand of gossip wasn't as threatening to her as the adult kind.

She allowed herself to listen to their more innocent speculations, to imagine what life would've been like if she had made a different choice so long ago and had turned her attention to D.J. instead of Dax.

Flash: she saw her and D.J. holding hands in a homecoming picture, both of them flushing pink, like the corsage on her wrist, and smiling until they looked a little tetched.

Flash: she saw the sparkle of an engagement ring as D.J. slid it onto her finger, saw the gem of a joyful tear as it ran down her face.

Flash: she saw herself in a wedding dress, kissing D.J. at the altar. Saw him holding her face in his hands as if she were the most precious element of his life.

A person who would do anything to keep their love strong.

She hadn't loved Dax enough to do that, and likewise, too. What would've happened if she'd loved D.J. instead? Would they be traveling the globe while she painted a view from every stop on their itinerary?

Would her parents still be proud because she'd succeeded in every possible respect?

Allaire wandered over to her Paris painting, uncovering it to find the blue of an oil-textured night, the gray of the distant streets under burning lamps.

Then she picked up her brush, thinking again of how D.J. had kissed her and given her a taste of a different, brighter world.

Chapter Seven

Meanwhile, outside Town Hall, D.J. found Russ Chilton shooting the breeze with a few other ranchers who'd been in the building earlier. D.J. had sat in the same auditorium, where the mayor had summoned citizens to discuss the changes Thunder Canyon was undergoing as well as expecting to undergo. From the peeved tones of Russ's group now, D.J. guessed that the meeting hadn't gone to their satisfaction.

When Russ spied his friend, he ambled over. "I saw you across the room, but I thought it'd be impolite to yell a hello at the time."

Russ attempted not to be obvious about checking out the fight-inflicted wounds that had forced D.J. to leave the Rib Shack's grand opening early. The cuts were healing nicely, but he still wore the odd bruise or two.

"I see you haven't fully recovered from that wood chipper accident," his friend said. "Dax is having the same problem."

Russ wasn't fooled, and D.J. knew he wouldn't be. But his old pal didn't push the subject, thank God.

The two of them headed toward their vehicles in the parking lot. A trace of sulfur threaded the air, as if holding it together with the threat of rain.

"I assume," Russ said, "you came to that meeting to get back into the community spirit?"

"I have a lot of catching up to do." D.J. didn't mention that the meeting had also provided a mental distraction from thinking of Allaire's kiss all day long.

Even as he still felt the soft pressure of her lips against his, he couldn't help wondering why it was taking her forever to return his call. Not that he'd been waiting by the phone the whole time, but he couldn't shake off the questions: Was she regretting their kiss enough to cut off all conversation with him? Was that the reason she'd run away after their intimate contact?

Had he blown their friendship apart?

See, this was what happened when a person put his emotions on the line, just as he'd wanted to do long ago. He'd been afraid that his feelings would alienate her and, now, his fears had come true.

But D.J. couldn't take any of it back. Hell, even if he went back across the country and tried to "improve" himself until the day he died, it might not be enough to ever win her over.

They were approaching a ramshackle pickup, Russ's latest tinkering project.

"Too bad I wasted my time here today," he said. "Always good to know that our mayor isn't doing a damned thing to stop all this so-called progress."

As they halted at Russ's door, the wind grew heavier, rustling the autumn-tinged trees and whistling an ominous tune.

D.J. watched Russ extract his keys from his waxed canvas coat. "Progress can't be that much of an enemy to Thunder Canyon. Every town evolves in some way or another."

"True, but some places do it slowly and

gracefully. You can't say that about our home-town, now, can you?"

D.J. thought about the flashy sports cars climbing up Thunder Mountain daily, thought about how he occasionally heard the rich tour-ists talking about investing in town property as they snacked at the Rib Shack.

"It'd be nice if things would slow down, I suppose," he said.

"And that isn't about to happen. Not any time soon, at this rate." Russ unlocked his door. "Sometimes change is more of a pre-lude to disaster than anything."

"Or sometimes change is a new beginning."

As his friend swung open his door, he cast an assessing glance at D.J. "Is that what you thought before you zoomed off to Georgia after high school? That change would bring about a whole new epoch for you?"

D.J. tried not to show how on target Russ was. Going to school in Atlanta had partly been D.J.'s way of altering what Allaire—and everyone else in Thunder Canyon—thought of him. Change was going to be his ally.

But that wasn't exactly how it'd turned out. Allaire's running away after the kiss wasn't a stamp of approval.

Russ continued. "Did trying to change your life really improve things all that much?"

A huff of wind moaned around D.J., chilling him. "I'm not too sure. All I know is that I had to try. If I didn't move around, I was going to atrophy."

"And, yet, I've never felt a case of that coming on, myself." Russ peered around, a wistful smile on his face. "A person ought to be willing to fight for what he already has."

The words pushed against D.J., as if seeking entrance. He knew he should embrace what Russ was saying, but he…couldn't. Not when he wanted more than he already had.

"See you at poker late Sunday?" D.J. asked, extending his hand.

They shook in parting, then went their separate ways.

As D.J. climbed into his own pickup, he saw Russ's battered truck hurtle past, his friend's hand lifted in farewell. With myriad squeaks that reminded D.J. of a comfortable old bed, the vehicle zoomed onto Main Street and then away.

D.J. waited for a few moments, the sky graying. As a few raindrops splattered on his windshield he considered what Russ had said.

A person ought to be willing to fight for what he already has.

Maybe D.J. should be thinking the same way. He'd been well on his way to reclaiming Allaire's friendship. In fact, he could've sworn that they'd pretty much picked up where they'd left off just before he'd gone to college—before she'd gotten married.

He'd *had* her companionship, but then he'd pushed it. He'd felt the compulsion to kiss her, to take what he'd wanted for so long.

Perhaps that hadn't been the right approach. He could've just stuck with what had been working. After all, having a friendly Allaire back in his life was much better than not having her at all.

If D.J. were smart, he would get his head together and just accept what he already possessed, as Russ advised.

As more raindrops tapped on his windshield, D.J. started his engine. It was cold and he would need some heat.

But Russ's words wouldn't dissipate.

Only a couple of nights ago, D.J. had claimed Allaire, if only for a short, sublime time. She'd kissed him as passionately as he'd kissed her, and no one could convince D.J. any differently of that.

Did he already *have* something besides her friendship? And, if he knew Allaire at all, he guessed that she could have been running from everything that went along with D.J. instead of merely fleeing from D.J. himself. She'd always been complex and over-analytical, but she had reason to be with what'd happened to her marriage.

Maybe there was more to her not calling D.J. back than he knew....

He released his parking brake and sped out of the lot, his windshield wipers brushing aside a rain that had started to fall in earnest.

If there was something he already *had* with Allaire besides their friendship, he couldn't let it go. Even if this was the biggest risk D.J. could ever take, he had to know, had to pursue it. He'd spent too much of his life hanging back.

Now it was time to suck it up and do something.

Hands tight on his wheel, he drove toward the high school, where he hoped Allaire would be winding up her day since she didn't have any pressing freelance jobs that he knew of.

And if she wasn't there?

Well, he'd think about that when the time called for it.

D.J. had wasted way too much of his energy second-guessing himself already.

After the students had left, Allaire had gone to the window, hearing the rain thudding against it. She was one of the few people on earth who'd never felt cozy on a rainy day. Maybe it was because, by nature, melancholy grated on her, even if it'd become such a big part of her recent life.

So she'd gone to her classroom boom box, where she often played Mozart for the kids, and inserted a CD mix that a student had burned for her. He'd discovered she was a TCHS graduate and had compiled a bunch of songs from her "ancient" school years, mainly as a joke.

But she loved the collection and often listened in her quiet hours. As "Macarena" came on, she lowered the volume, then settled in to work on her painting.

Cheesy memories could be good company.

She experimented with adding more vivid color to the Paris nightscape, and it pleased her so much that she sat back and imagined she was there, in the City of Lights.

The glow reminded her of how D.J.'s eyes brightened when he saw her, of how he'd shown such fire in his gaze the night they'd kissed.

She felt his skin scratch over her cheek again, felt the warmth of lips that belonged against hers. He'd felt so perfect pressed against her body, like a portion of her that had floated away and had come back as if it'd never left.

When she heard a voice break into her musings, she startled, her heart blasting into a thousand flutters that immediately flew back together again.

"If they played this kind of junk at prom," the voice behind her said, "I'm sure glad I missed it."

D.J.

Was this a part of the fantasy or…?

Her pulse was still buzzing from her reverie, almost like the wings of a hummingbird as it flew in one place, feeding. She held on to his voice for a moment—just a decadent second that she knew couldn't last—and exhaled. But she wasn't obvious about it.

Her stomach somersaulted as she turned in

her chair to face him. He still carried injuries from the fight with Dax and, although they'd mellowed, she could still imagine them under her fingertips. She'd wanted so badly to erase his pain.

Should she say something about not calling him?

Or should she stick to the harmless subject of prom? Then again, she'd gone with Dax to two of them. D.J. had stayed home both times.

She went with another option.

"Did you need a place to dry off?" she asked, making light of his wet hair and skin.

The normal D.J. would've grinned at her amiable comment, but he seemed so serious. That scared her.

Thrilled her.

He shut the door behind him and Allaire's heartbeat really took off.

"I wanted to stop by to see you," he said.

"Voice mail message," she blurted, wanting to stop him before he said too much about how she'd avoided him after their kiss. "I've been meaning to return your call, but..."

D.J. took a step forward, his gaze steady and seemingly determined. Oh, God, that scared— and thrilled—her most of all.

"But what, Allaire?"

His tone was soft, so gentle that she *wanted* to turn away so he wouldn't know he'd flipped her life topsy-turvy.

Yet she didn't move. Lord knew, she'd wanted him to come after her, to force her to admit what she was feeling.

If that's why he was here...

Just as she was about to tell D.J. how mixed up she was, another song poured out of the boom box—"Because You Loved Me," by Celine Dion. It'd been the theme of her senior prom, and she and Dax had danced to it after she'd been crowned queen. Both she and D.J. had been on the yearbook staff, and she recalled how he'd managed to avoid working on that page when he'd been asked by their advisor.

It was as if he...

As if he'd wished he was in that picture instead of Dax.

D.J. had obviously noted the song, too, because he tipped back his head, a rueful smile on his lips. Then, shaking his head, he shed his coat, hanging it over a chair so it would dry off.

Allaire felt as if she'd been granted a reprieve.

"More dorky prom songs," she said to smooth out the moment.

"They probably weren't so dorky when you were in your dress, out on the floor with the rest of the kids. I'll bet you knew the words to every slow song, and you believed them, too."

She had a vague recollection of that—of living a ballad every day. But that was puppy love, right? Rainbows, hearts and starry lyrics that you wanted to emulate.

"I wonder," she said, nestling her paintbrush in a cup near her easel, "when we officially start thinking these kinds of songs are 'dorky.'"

"When our hearts first break?" he asked.

She forced a laugh, still feeling the pressure of what they weren't talking about suffocate the room. "I think you just came up with the title of a number one hit."

What she couldn't say out loud was, *When did* your *heart first break, D.J.? And who did it to you?*

She wanted to know everything, even in spite of herself.

Silence descended, but she didn't allow it to linger for even another second.

"So how goes life at the Rib Shack?" she

asked, moving to the classroom sink to clean off her hands.

"The Shack?" He said it as if he couldn't believe she was asking about something so trivial.

"I heard you've been booked since the opening. Congrats."

"Thanks." He paused. "Allaire, I—"

"Where are you planning to open the next Shack?"

Desperate. She was so desperate to put him off.

"Trying to drive me out of town already?" he asked. "I haven't been here all that long."

"No, that's not…" She faced him, drying off her hands.

He was raising an eyebrow, probably in an attempt to look less hurt than she guessed he was. His eyes couldn't hide the damage she'd already done.

"That's not what I meant at all, D.J." Sick of herself, she tossed the towel near the sink.

Here it was—another moment of truth. She could feel it pulling and pushing at her.

As another song came on—"Un-Break My Heart" by Toni Braxton—D.J. rolled up his sleeves. His forearms were stranded with muscle, and the sight of them sent a naughty rush through Allaire.

He'd turned into such a man....

"If I didn't know any better," he said, moving toward her, "I'd say you were in a time warp with this music."

"It's a mix from a student. He was probably trying to get on my good side."

As D.J. came closer, Allaire's mouth went dry, her pulse slamming through her veins.

That kiss, she thought. That kiss had been a twist in her complacency, and she craved more of it.

D.J.'s voice lowered. "I'd guess that your male CD-burning student might have a crush on his teacher."

"That's not true, D—"

The words caught in her throat as he stood before her. So warm, so tempting. She could barely think straight with him being so near.

His tone went gritty. "It would've been nice to have had one dance at the prom."

She self-imploded, her skin flaring, then sucking into a flash of yearning.

While she took a step backward, reaching behind so she could steady herself with the counter, D.J. grasped her other hand. As usual, he balanced her, even as her mind went spinning and reeling.

At the heat of his skin, Allaire forgot the reason she'd run away from him in the first place. It didn't seem to matter that she was falling for her ex's brother.

Nothing mattered right now but D.J.'s hand holding hers.

The world went hazy, like a night washed with silver stars hanging from a gym's ceiling. As D.J. rested his other hand on her waist, she found herself placing her palm on his wide shoulder.

The dance he'd never had.

She'd gone pliant, and he relaxed, then smiled until her knees went weak.

"I had a talk with Russ today," he said, apropos of nothing. But knowing D.J., he was getting around to saying something important.

Allaire made a sound that could've meant anything. Anything at all.

They were truly dancing now, slowly, hesitantly.

"He got me to thinking." D.J. frowned slightly. "Thinking about change. About why keeping things the same could be for the best."

Keeping things the same, Allaire thought.

Was D.J. talking about staying friends? She wasn't so sure, not with them swaying to a song full of longing.

Not with her inching closer to him by the moment.

In fact, her chest brushed his, creating friction that rolled to a wall of heat covering her entire body.

But she didn't back away. Not now.

"If things never changed between the two of us," D.J. added, "we wouldn't run the risk of disrespecting Dax, right? And I wouldn't have to worry about losing my best friend."

"We could never stop caring about each other, D.J."

He stopped their cautious rhythm, coming to pin her down with an intent look.

"Is that true, Allaire? No matter what happens, you'd always stick with me? You'd never run off on me again?"

"I…didn't know what else to do that night," she said, her hold tightening on his hand. "I got away from you before…"

"Before what?"

She didn't know what to say.

Before she could take the kiss to the next level? Before she could tell D.J. that seeing him again would encourage too much of a stir and, hence, make her life more uncomfortable than it already was?

Before she could risk goofing up yet again?

D.J. took both her hands in his, bringing them to his chest. There, she could feel his pulse pounding. Her own matched it bang for bang.

"I'm tired of never saying what's in my heart," he said. "I'm tired of never taking a stand. And I'm not going to be the quiet guy anymore."

Blood rushed to her head. How should she deal with this? What could she…?

Relationships never work out, Arianna would've said. *I don't know why you even bothered with Dax.*

Allaire didn't want to hear whatever D.J. was about to say…didn't—

But D.J. had already steeled himself.

"I've always loved you, Allaire, and now that I'm back, I know that I always will."

Chapter Eight

Even though the aftermath of D.J.'s confession pressed in on him, robbing him of oxygen, he didn't want to take it back. He was through with tiptoeing around and denying his real feelings.

Done.

But when he saw the utter shock on Allaire's face, his will almost gave out.

She was speechless, and that couldn't be a good thing. A hesitation to speak could only go on for so long before it led to awful news.

Was it too late to take it back, after all?

In the background, the boom box started

pummeling out a rap song. Okay, maybe it wasn't *pummeling,* but it sure sounded like it in this endlessly mortifying moment. The rain against the windows was even too damned loud, because every drop felt like a second guess pounding away at his skull.

Why the hell did you say it, D.J.? Damn it, isn't this kind of reaction the reason you shut up about your real feelings in the first place? You were right about staying mum.

But now it was too late.

When Allaire still didn't respond, he stalked over to the boom box and snapped it off.

That left the raindrops to do their nattering, but D.J. couldn't shut those off, too. God knew he wished he could silence everything, especially all the doubts gnawing at him.

After a moment, Allaire finally covered her face with her hands, as if to block him out.

Doubts or not, he'd had it. "You're acting like I told you the sky is falling."

"I don't mean to. It's just…" She removed her hands, revealing flushed skin.

Was she mortified, too?

D.J. hoped he was wrong. These past days, he thought he'd seen a lot of proof that she felt something, as well.

He calmed himself, gentling his voice in spite of an urge to stay angry in the face of yet another rejection.

"Then what *is* it, Allaire? Talk to me."

She wrapped her arms around herself, and D.J. knew from experience that she was going into her own little defensively comfortable world. "I'm not the same person I was all those years ago. You can't be in love with someone who doesn't exist now. Actually, I…I don't know who I am at all anymore, D.J.…."

"Yes, you do." He gestured toward the Paris painting, noticing that she'd added color to the intricate, yet subdued rendering. It was a good change. "You're the same Allaire who had me smitten years ago."

D.J. didn't think it was possible, but her skin got even redder. She looked like a woman who didn't know which way to turn, because every angle presented a truth she obviously didn't want to confront.

"Allaire, I *know* you." He wanted to go to her, but that might chase her off for good this time, so he stayed his ground. "Who else knows about all those dreams you used to have? And who else knows that not reaching them made you so sad? You can't tell me that anyone else really understands how much you wanted to see your work in a New York gallery someday. You can't tell me that anyone else knows how many paintings you started and abandoned because they just weren't showing what was inside that brilliant mind of yours. Who else knows that you've got a secret art graveyard in the corner of your parents' back field?"

From the wistful look in her eyes, D.J. could tell that no one knew but him.

He finally moved toward her, carefully. "Even if we spent a lot of time apart, I know the real you."

At that, her knuckles went white as she gripped herself harder. "Yeah, the *real* me. Aren't you proud of how many of my dreams actually came true, D.J.? Don't you have to wonder if *any* of my goals will ever be reached?"

Her fragile mask had dropped, revealing a side D.J. had been privy to long ago—a side she hadn't shown recently. But he loved this less idealistic part of her, also.

Loved everything about her.

"How many people become what they dreamed of when they were younger, anyway?" he asked.

But she was stridently firing off more, as if her words could keep him at bay. He knew it was the only way she could cope with the bombshell he'd just laid on her.

Patient, he thought. *Keep handling her with care.*

"Listen to you—the successful one." Allaire's voice was thick by now, evidence of just how vital all those ambitions had been to her, and how much it had hurt when she'd failed to realize them. "*You* made something of yourself, so how can you sit there and say you understand?"

He was close enough now to reach out and touch her cheek. When he made contact, Allaire skittishly retreated.

But D.J. wasn't going to ignore the truth anymore.

With tender persuasion, he cupped her jaw in both his hands, his thumbs resting under her cheekbones. Her skin was burning, and he attempted to stroke the fever away.

"I never dreamed of owning restaurants," he whispered, blood crashing through him. "My dreams had everything to do with you, Allaire, and until the other night, none of them had ever come true."

As his meaning registered with her, images of their kiss consumed D.J. He risked getting even closer, a whisper away from her mouth. Memory slipped into reality as he determined to make that first kiss into a second one....

Their lips melded, and she tasted of every fantasy he'd nurtured. He pulled away to see if she was just as unable to resist as he was.

"D.J.," she whispered, gaze clouded.

It was an entreaty, an invitation from a woman, not a girl.

A woman who filled him up in a way successful business ventures or money could never do.

When she tentatively touched a scab near his eye, a souvenir from the fight with Dax, D.J. shuddered. It didn't hurt. Actually, it was more the hungry heat in her stare that was slicing him.

Allaire parted her lips and ran her gaze to his mouth, and D.J. realized she was offering another invitation. He took control, just as he should've done in the beginning, back when he was a kid daydreaming in class about her.

He coasted one of his hands to the back of her head, cradling her as he claimed her lips again. His kiss was harder now, starving, and he devoured her in a bid to make up for lost time.

A tiny moan came from low in her throat, and she pressed her hands to his waist, then up his back, urging him toward her.

Sparked, D.J. obeyed her subtle demand, fitting himself against her, body to body. He could feel her breasts, her belly, all of her warm and willing.

His nether regions awakened, pulsing to hardness. Allaire nestled against him, angling her head back and disconnecting from his lips to breathe out a harsh sigh.

This was going so fast, he thought. Fast enough to warp his common sense. His body screamed, "Go," but something inside him that had always guarded his fantasies about Allaire begged him to stop.

Take it slow.

Take it easy.

But there was a gleam in her eyes, a craving. She pulled him back down to kiss her again, and D.J. was all but helpless to say no.

With the force of their passion, they stumbled back, nudging her desk. Now, she was devouring *him,* and that wiped out any thoughts of holding back.

Allaire wanted him. It was almost too much to fold his mind around.

But his body had no such problems with comprehension. He slid his tongue past her lips, deepening the kiss, drawing it out into long strokes, lazy nips and sucks. In his excitement, his erection brushed her belly, and she gasped, tightening her grip on his back.

This is what it's like to feel her, D.J. thought. *Is this even real? Or are you imagining it again?*

It was real. And mind-blowing. Their first kiss had only been a preview—this was everything.

His body pounded, blinding him with flashes of heat. He was near to bursting and, in a split second of clarity, D.J. realized that if he wasn't careful, all his pent-up fantasizing was going to explode in a rushed minute.

"Wait," he said. "Wait, Allaire…"

She was running a hand over his chest now, enticing him, deaf to what he was saying.

"Allaire…"

With a grand effort, he pulled away, holding her hands while trying to find his normal breathing rhythm again. Damn it, it wouldn't be long until he lost all control.…

Allaire was breathing heavily, too, and it took a moment for her gaze to focus. When it did, she seemed bewildered by his reluctance to continue.

"The last thing I want," he said, "is to hurry something that I've spent years building up in my mind."

At first, she frowned, but then understanding dawned. "Oh."

"I want every bit of this to be special." Now *he* flushed. "I'd like to think I had more control, Allaire, but…"

"But you've been imagining what it'd be like to be with me ever since you were old enough to put together a proper scenario?"

"Pretty much." He drew back a few inches. Safer here. At least a little.

The distance allowed him to even out his pulse, but that didn't mean his nethers weren't complaining loud and clear. He clenched his jaw and sat at a seat behind a table. Hiding his arousal didn't erase it, but he was determined to wait for the perfect night, the perfect time— and from the way she'd kissed him again, from the way she wasn't running off this time, he knew it was going to happen.

Maybe his confidence was stoked by the

dreamy way she was watching him. Maybe it was because she couldn't help touching her lips, as if still feeling a kiss buzz over their softness.

Seeing her in such a state didn't do much to quell D.J.'s desire. He would have to stay sitting for a while.

"Why didn't you say anything back then?" she asked.

"Besides the fact that you were with Dax?" D.J. leaned his forearms on the table. "I loved you even before that, Allaire. But I never had the courage to see what would happen if you knew. My time ran out when Dax noticed you, and I never got another chance."

She finally dropped her hand from her mouth. "And no matter how much you two didn't get along, you would never hurt him. That's understandable, D.J. I just can't believe you never—"

"I came close." D.J. followed a wood grain on the desk with a finger. "There was one night that seemed ripe for the telling, but...I couldn't."

"When was that?"

It all rushed back. The summer night before D.J. had left for college. He had invited

Allaire to go for one last meandering car ride through the country. She'd thought it would just be another outing where they would talk, hang out, enjoy each other's company while Dax worked on his bikes and she joined him later for a real date.

But D.J. had been intending all the while to open his heart.

However, when they'd arrived at their favorite "talking spot" on a remote road, then parked under an aged, massive oak tree, he came to his senses.

Or, more appropriately, he'd chickened out yet again.

Now that D.J. thought about it, he knew that this one night could've changed everything, for better or for worse.

D.J. told her the details, measuring her reaction, wondering if she'd ever possessed any hint of how her best friend had truly felt about her. Then he waited, knowing from just watching her that she genuinely hadn't realized anything back then.

"I remember that night," she said. "How you seemed distracted. You kept toying with the graduation hat tassel hanging from your rearview mirror. You always got fidgety when you were uncomfortable. You still do."

"Not much has changed about me. I still want you in my life more than anything, too."

A pause stretched, needled by raindrops on the window.

"What about Dax?" she finally asked.

"What about him?"

Allaire sighed, probably because there was nothing else to say. Or maybe there was too much.

Standing, D.J. wasn't about to lose what he'd gained tonight. Hell, no. Even though he knew they weren't going to jump into a new relationship headfirst—getting used to what this evening had brought on would take time—he was going to hang on like a damned bulldog.

"Allaire, we could be discreet right now, until everyone eases into the idea of us being together. Then…"

"D.J., don't be unrealistic."

"Unrealistic is thinking that you're not going to want me to kiss you again."

She blinked, and it probably just wasn't at the straightforwardness of his comment. She *had* to recognize her feelings. He'd seen how strongly she felt about him in her eyes, sensed how much she wanted him, too, from her body.

"So what're we going to do?" he asked.

"We're…" She blew out a breath, then straightened up, standing away from the desk. "I don't know, D.J. I really don't know."

But *he* knew. She was afraid of gossip right now and, even though Dax had acknowledged their attraction, D.J. knew Allaire would have to work up to it.

"Well, I'll tell you, then," he said. "We're going to see each other later tonight, after the Shack closes. You can come over to add a couple of details to the mural—it's a good excuse to be around me if you need one—and…" No hesitation, no more fading away into the background. "And we'll go from there."

He almost expected her to cross her arms over her body again, to get defensive, but she didn't. Instead, she lay a hand over her tummy, as if feeling things there that she couldn't ignore.

A banging sound erupted from the school's hallway, reminding D.J. of where they were. That he and Allaire weren't alone in their own universe.

"That'd be Mr. Ozzel," she said softly. "He's making the rounds."

"Then I'd best get to the Shack before the rush."

He stood there for a moment, wondering if it would be okay to kiss her, to tide himself over with one small hint of what could happen later. It was going to be a long night waiting for her.

But Allaire was already behind her desk, opening drawers. She tossed him a smile, which slowly melted to a secretive, shy grin.

She was thinking about their kiss. Thinking about tonight.

D.J. *knew* it.

As he left, he walked with a slight swagger, probably looking like a man who'd just wrapped the world up and put it in his pocket to later give to the woman he loved.

D.J. made it past Mr. Ozzel without being seen and was almost beyond the office when reality bit him.

Mrs. Fleitchman, a secretary who still wore her graying hair in a bob and her glasses on a silver neck chain, was locking up. She glanced briefly at D.J. while she wrestled with her keys.

"Nice to see you, Dax."

He couldn't move. Literally. He had no idea

how she'd mixed up him and his brother. Maybe it was the confidence that had marked D.J.'s steps. The confidence that'd just drained right out of him.

When he corrected her and she put on her lenses to laugh and say she was sorry, he started thinking too much. It was his curse.

Because the more D.J. thought, the more his rosy glow rubbed off to reveal something lingering underneath the happiness. Something that was bound to be an issue.

Now that the intensity of their kisses had ebbed, was Allaire thinking past the dizzy moment, too?

Was she comparing D.J. to Dax?

He tried to stop himself from mulling over it, but now the question of how D.J. measured up to his older, cooler brother wouldn't go away.

Would it ever?

Later that night, before Allaire entered the Rib Shack, she called D.J.'s cell to tell him she was there.

"It's near midnight," he said, "and I kicked everyone out except for the night steward. He's got to clean and prep for tomorrow, so maybe we can grab a snack here and then…?"

He left the possibilities hanging, but she barely heard any of it. D.J.'s voice had that much of an effect, seeping into her and stirring her up again.

He loved her. Said he had for a long, long time. The realization addled her, made her smile, made her laugh and want to hold the knowledge inside so it would never turn out to be untrue.

At the same time, his confession frightened her to death. What was she supposed to do with the information? What if she gave in to her every instinct to be with him and she blew it, just as she had with Dax?

Lastly, how would D.J.—her D.J.—fit into her life if he wasn't just a pal anymore?

She was having trouble reconciling the old and the new. Actually, it was more than that. She was struggling to decide just how far she should allow him inside.

If he got too far, and things didn't work out…

Okay, this defeatist attitude wasn't what she wanted to feel at all. D.J. had kissed her again, and she'd given as good as she'd gotten. And she'd wanted more. That's why she was here, right?

To pursue more?

She locked up her Jeep, then walked toward the Rib Shack's front entrance while surveying the parking lot. It was nearly empty, save for D.J.'s red pickup and an old sports car—probably belonging to the steward. Asphalt, wet from that night's earlier rain, smelled sharp in her nostrils, but that was balanced by the cleansing scent of the nearby pine trees.

In the distance, she heard people laughing as they came out of the lodge's shopping hall entrance, and she went on alert. Her pulse hammered until she told herself to cool it.

Why should she be feeling like a bad girl for sneaking inside the Shack? She'd been divorced for four years, and Dax was over her. Would he really care if she was on her way to see D.J.?

If she was on her way to see if they should take their kisses to another level?

She recalled the other night, when the brothers had fought. Recalled how Dax had uttered, "Just open your eyes and do what you need to *now,* you brick-head," as a parting shot to D.J.

His comment could've meant a thousand things, but Allaire couldn't shake the suspicion that Dax had also noticed how she'd been watching D.J. from across the room that night. Everyone had probably noticed.

Her stride slowed as she rethought what she was about to do.

What would the town think? And how many times would Arianna say, "You're trying again, even after the first disaster?"

Following the divorce, Allaire had felt idiotic enough around her sister, even though her older sibling hadn't made a show of how pleased she was that the golden girl could be human, too. Still, Allaire had definitely been taken down a peg.

Was she ready to be taken down another one if things with D.J. didn't work out?

Just in case, she took out a few brushes from her art bag as she climbed the stairs to the Shack's outside entrance. If anyone saw her going inside, she would flash her supplies and claim that she was doing touch-ups after a late night of schoolwork. She'd done the same with the *Thunder Canyon Cowboys* set pieces, so the excuse wouldn't be far-fetched.

She opened the restaurant's door and peered inside. "Hello?"

D.J.'s voice came from the back. "Be right out!"

Shutting the door, Allaire contained a quiver at hearing him. Her new D.J.

She thought about how, earlier, he'd altered every perception she'd had about him. Even that wound by his eye had done something to her. It wasn't so much that he'd fought Dax… Oh, no. It was more that the injury brought out a raw side of him, a part he'd kept hidden. Although the old D.J. would always warm her heart, this one stimulated every nerve ending until it sang. This one had gotten her to drop everything and kiss him senseless.

Jeez, she was out of control. Where had her restraint gone?

As if to find answers, she wandered over to her mural. She smiled, kind of proud about how it'd turned out. Okay, very proud. She could hardly even believe that she'd accomplished such a feat….

The images ensnared her, especially the ones she'd embedded in the bigger Thunder Canyon pictures. Her fantasy trip.

The Tower of London, the Loch Ness… They were the only constants in her life. Even D.J. had changed tonight, and she wasn't sure he was so safe anymore….

She didn't know how long she looked at that

mural before she felt D.J.'s presence. But as she turned to find him standing against a nearby pillar, her heart knocked against her chest.

"Hi, again," she said softly, already wanting another kiss.

"Why don't you get on over here, Allaire."

Her skin seemed to ruffle, to become ultra aware. Barely able to walk, she managed to go over to him, anyway, drawn by this new assurance of his, calmed by the hope that he would never do anything to let her down. But...

Never trust any of them, Arianna had once told her.

And, not long ago, Allaire had wondered if her sister hadn't been too far off the mark.

But this was D.J. Not Dax. Not any other man in this world, either.

Standing before him now, Allaire tucked a strand of her hair behind an ear. She'd taken her more conservative style down when she'd gone home to shower, and had never put it back up.

He reached out to take a lock between his fingers. "I love when you wear it down like this."

Before she knew what she was doing, she leaned forward on her tiptoes, capturing his lips with hers.

Their heartbeats punched at each other, as if testing and gauging. Then, their pulses sped up, coming into sync.

But she felt a difference in D.J., a hesitation.

He drew back slightly, resting his forehead against hers while enfolding her in his arms, taking away the strain of her having to balance on tiptoe.

Disappointment flooded her. She wasn't sure what had just happened.

"I never suspected you were such a great kisser," she said, trying to encourage him to start again.

He paused, and she would've given her left arm to know exactly what he was thinking.

Finally, he grinned. A slightly troubled grin. "I had a lot of time to muse about how I'd perfect my technique."

"Well, it worked."

His gaze darkened even more.

"What's wrong?" she asked.

D.J. seemed to brace himself. "I'm done talking around things, Allaire, so I'm just going to say it. I know you're going to tell me I'm being ridiculous, but I can't help wondering if maybe, in the back of your mind, you can't help comparing me to—"

"No," she said flatly. Did Dax even have to interfere with this, their most private of moments?

She tightened her grip on D.J.'s hands. "I'm glad you mentioned it, but you're right—it's ridiculous for you to believe I'd be thinking of Dax while we're kissing. He wasn't meant for me. You obviously were."

"That's what I keep telling myself, too, but…"

"Listen to me, D.J. When you kiss me, I'm so overwhelmed that I can't think of *anything,* much less my ex-husband."

A bashful moment seemed to catch him, but when she smiled, he pulled her into another kiss.

Allaire couldn't have said how long it lasted because minutes lost definition. But when their intimacy heated—mostly because she initiated it by untucking his flannel shirt—D.J. slowed down.

"When the time comes," he said, "I want it to last. Right now, I feel like I'm heading for a quick crash."

Allaire knew he was right. Dang it all, they couldn't just fall into bed and expect things to work out. They had too much history to sort through. Besides, as much as she wanted him, she needed to be cautious.

He recognized her frustration. "I just need to get used to this and stop feeling like a school bus that has no brakes."

"Me, too," she said. "I mean…I know I came here tonight thinking…" She laughed, knowing she should just come right out with it. "Thinking we'd be taking up where we left off with kissing. But really, D.J.? Slow sounds really good to me. Just *kissing* you is throwing me into a dither right now, and going slow means that we can get comfortable with all this craziness."

Slow also meant that she'd have plenty of time to recognize if things weren't working out….

But her problem was this: she hadn't experienced physical release since splitting from Dax. She'd packed her sex drive away and, like a coiled spring, it was ready to be let loose.

Especially now that she knew how D.J. had always felt about her. That got to her most of all in a poignant, heart-twisting way.

"Whatever you need, Allaire." He kissed her once more, as if savoring her, then headed toward the kitchen. "I guess I've got a date with some cold water. You need a drink? And do you want a snack?"

She wasn't hungry for food. "Water. Just water sounds good."

As he left, she thunked into a chair, weak yet stimulated. So there wouldn't be any pressure to go beyond kisses tonight. She was relieved, and she hated feeling that way. Fear was keeping her libido in check, fear of fumbling.

And the longer he took, the more their earlier conversation started getting to her.

I can't help wondering if maybe, in the back of your mind, you can't help comparing me to—

Allaire tugged at her skirt, trying to keep her inner Arianna from ruining the rest of tonight. But her older sister's voice acted as an unwelcome conscience, anyway.

Do you think D.J. might be using you to compete with Dax, even if it isn't intentional?

The notion was so ludicrous that Allaire even physically swatted it away.

Wasn't it?

Uh, *yes.* Furthermore, instead of dreaming up dumb ways to sabotage a relationship that had barely even started, Allaire should be attempting to make it up to D.J. for not recognizing how he'd felt about her. How could she have missed that?

She heard D.J.'s footsteps and faced him.

He was holding two bottles of water, an expression of such profound affection on his face that her heart couldn't help but jerk to a halt.

Had he always looked at her like this? Or was he just allowing himself to show it now?

Either way, Allaire wondered if she could ever make him as happy as she had in his dreams.

Chapter Nine

A few late nights later, D.J. gunned his pickup onto Winterhawk Lane, near the county line. In the passenger seat, Allaire gave a little squeal.

"Where did you learn to drive like this?" she asked, laughing.

"It came with maturity."

He slowed the vehicle down, his headlights saturating the white fences lining the remote road. Gnarled trees pasted themselves against the moonlit sky, reminding D.J. of how, as a kid, he'd torn construction paper in his own art class and made ragged collages out of the pieces. Teachers like Allaire enjoyed having their students create those things.

D.J. took another road corner, more gently this time. Speaking of Allaire's teaching, it seemed as if staying up after the Rib Shack's closing hours to have these "discreet" meetings that he'd been banking on for her comfort, and *then* having to go into work early, was taking a lot out of her. Often, late at night after they'd settled in D.J.'s cabin to watch old movies, she would fall asleep in his arms.

Hell, at least his cuddling was that comfortable to her—it seemed that innocent canoodling was what she needed right now. A smooth transition from best friend to boyfriend. Too bad he wasn't getting the chance to find out what effect anything beyond cuddling and kissing would have on her, though....

Allaire's voice eased him back to the moment. "Do you remember how far out the Post is?"

"Maybe ten minutes from here."

She was referring to Fort Donaugh, a small historical site where kids used to hang out on weekend nights. Having taken the night off, he was taking her to the old Trading Post because she needed inspiration for an upcoming art lesson plan. Tomorrow after school, she would be meeting with a history teacher on staff because they wanted to "teach across the curriculum." The plan was for the kids to choose a local spot that "spoke" to them and then base an art project on their impressions; they would also have to research their site and complete a report for history. Since Allaire wanted to model how the artistic part of the project would work for her students, here she was, enlisting D.J.'s help in mining the old Trading Post for an example.

But there was another reason they'd come out here to the fringes of Thunder Canyon, too, D.J. thought. Because it wasn't daylight and it wasn't in town, where people could comment on their being together.

He tightened his grip on the steering wheel, wondering how the teenaged D.J. would've reacted if he'd known that, ten years in the future, he would be courting Allaire. That they would be working their way up to getting her past a certain gun-shyness and into D.J.'s arms for good.

But he hadn't expected the courting to be *this* tough. And he wasn't just talking about Allaire's slow acceptance of their feelings, either. A flickering resentment for Dax was still dogging D.J. because her divorce from his brother was only adding to her perfection complex, and that was what was holding her back from committing.

The sibling rivalry had only gotten worse in D.J.'s mind.

In fact, the other night, when he'd told her about how he wondered if she was comparing him to Dax, he'd thought that would be the extent of the issue. Instead, bringing the subject to light had resurrected the competitive streak in D.J. After kissing her again and again, he found himself hoping that he lived up to his brother's proficient reputation. He found himself striving to win any small victory over Dax.

But why was he allowing himself to dwell on it? D.J. loved Allaire and he suspected that, someday, if he tried his best, she would feel the same way.

It *should've* been that simple.

D.J. pulled to the side of the road, where the historical site was chained off from the public. Tonight, there were no cars parked near the embankment or nestled among the trees.

"All alone," he said, cutting the engine.

Allaire bashfully glanced at him, then leaned over for a soft kiss. It was as if she'd painted thick strokes over his vision, whiting it out as her lips branded his.

"Sorry for dragging you out here," she murmured against his mouth. "We should be tucked away at your place."

He took her lower lip between both of his, toying with her, nipping and teasing. Allaire rested her hand on his arm, as if anchoring herself.

He wished they were tucked away at home. But…slow. That's how he would win Allaire over. He had to remember that, no matter how badly he wanted to make up for all the time he'd lost with her.

Allaire caressed his face, then tweaked his chin as she disengaged. "We've got work to do."

She grinned, pulling on her gloves and scarf, then hopped out of the pickup. D.J. groaned, half out of sexual frustration, half out of resignation.

Another one of those nights with her scuttling away and him soldiering after her.

He alighted from the pickup, too, fixing his coat so that it would keep out the cold. While they traipsed up to the gate, Allaire tugged a light blue stocking cap over her unbound hair.

The air had a definite nip to it as he took her hand and led her around the metal structure.

The trail led them to the night-hushed Trading Post, a small log structure standing in the middle of a clearing. Around them, fallen leaves held glinting beer cans, mementos of those teenaged weekend gatherings.

D.J. idly set to picking up some of the trash as his girlfriend took out a sketchpad and removed one of her gloves so she could draw properly.

Yup, *girlfriend.* He'd gone and thought it.

Automatically, D.J.'s subconscious asked, *What would Dax have to say about* that?

Even as D.J. tried to shove off the thought, he got a certain satisfaction out of this irony: Dax had never minded when D.J. had done homework with Allaire or when they'd taken their "cruises" after school and on weekend evenings. As long as D.J. relinquished her later in the night, after Mr. Stud Muffin finished tooling around with his bikes, Dax had no problem with his brother hanging around with his girl. He'd never considered D.J. a threat.

D.J. continued fetching more cans and, soon, he had his hands full. Allaire finished her quick sketch and noticed his collection.

"Oh, my, nature boy," she said. "You do keep America clean."

D.J. chuckled. "You ready to leave yet?"

"Aw, are you too cold? The South spoiled you with its more temperate weather, didn't it? Where's the guy who used to run around in the snow without his jacket?"

"He got hauled back inside by his father and chewed out." It seemed like yesterday when Dad had paid attention only when D.J. pulled the occasional dumb maneuver. Not that he performed many of those. D.J. walked the straight and narrow. But he could admit that when his father *did* notice a bum move and cared enough to get on D.J.'s case about it, the attention had been like a strange reward. The reminder that Dad still cared had kept D.J. hoping that a chewing out would turn into more time spent together.

Warped but true.

After putting away her sketchpad, Allaire turned her face to the sky, seeming to appreciate the openness, the romance of a clear night. He lost himself in her enjoyment.

Then she spoke. "I've been putting it all together."

Okay. Apropos of nothing, but he would go with it.

"Putting what together?" he asked.

"You."

D.J. leisurely walked toward her, and she came out of her reverie, strolling to meet him halfway.

"This place makes me feel like we've gone back to the old days," she said. "It makes me vividly recall the way you used to act around me…" She took a few cans from him. "It makes more sense now."

Without a word, they fell into step, their boots crunching over dirt and deadened autumn grass.

She continued. "I always thought you were too shy to ask anyone out. But then, when a girl would do the asking for you, you *still* didn't bother to date."

When D.J. opened his mouth to argue the point, she didn't let him.

"What about when both Alicia Hopkins and Karen Montemagni asked you to go with them to the Sadie Hawkins dance? You didn't. And there were other years when you were asked, too, D.J."

"Dances. Who needed them." Truthfully,

he hadn't gone because there was no point in being with someone who wasn't Allaire. He also hadn't had the stomach to endure the sight of her dancing with a guy who wasn't him.

"And you never had a steady girlfriend," she added. "Even when *I* set you up with Didi Barker for a movie date, you didn't seem interested."

"Yeah, by the way, I'd like to thank you for that again. Didi kept talking about her ex-boyfriend all night."

"So you weren't compatible."

"I knew what I wanted." He grinned at her. "*Who* I wanted."

A flash of pure desire lit her gaze and, for a moment, D.J. thought about dropping everything and pulling her into his arms right then and there. Forget all this "working up to the big moment" stuff.

He almost did it, too, except for the abrupt flap and cry of a bird as it burst out of the foliage above them.

Allaire froze.

But then the bird fluttered away, winging down to the nearby, tree-hidden road.

Although she recovered, acting as if nothing had happened, D.J. couldn't stop a twist of frustration from tightening his chest.

"Don't worry," he said, "the bird won't tell anyone that we're together."

She still didn't say anything.

Hell, she didn't have to—not when she'd made it clear that the threat of the town labeling her a man-eater—no, make that a *brother*-eater—was more important than shouting to the world that she had feelings for D.J.

He wasn't sure what those feelings were, exactly, but he was working on it.

"Allaire," he said, "somebody in town is going to find out about us sooner or later."

"Tori's privy to what's going on. But she'll never tell."

"And that's so very important, because if anyone were ever to discover how scandalous you are, it'd be the end of the world."

"Don't, D.J."

"Don't what? Say the truth?"

Allaire came to a halt just before the gate. The spikes of pine tree needles caught the moon's glow and cast sharp shadows over half her face.

"You wouldn't be the one they're judging," she said.

The comment struck him upside the head, ringing in his ears. "Why's that? Because nobody ever expected me to be anything more than the lesser brother? Because I never had any big standards to live up to in this town, unlike you?"

He shouldn't have said it, but the buried sentiment was out there, uncovered yet still crusted with his angst.

"I'm sorry, Allaire," he said, wishing he could do more than just apologize. "That was wrong."

"No, you're right." She sighed. "You've been patient with me. You've even arranged these secret meetings for us. I knew what you were doing, and I appreciate it. It's natural for you to be upset."

He started to placate her, as was his engrained habit, but she wouldn't have it.

"Just…don't make excuses for me. We're beyond that—or at least we have to get beyond that at this stage of our lives. You *should* challenge my neuroses. It's what I need. I won't grow out of them if there isn't someone like you to help me."

She shifted, and the shadow lifted from her face, giving him a clear view of her pale skin, her wide blue eyes.

There went his heart again, going hot and then scalding him all the way through.

"And you should challenge me, too," he said, wanting so badly to make her feel better. "If it weren't for you, I might never have approached Dax."

"You might never have gotten bruised up by him, as well, thanks to me." She lavished a gaze over his face, where his wounds were fainter reminders of the fistfight.

They tentatively smiled at each other, and D.J. was so taken with her that he almost forgot she'd wheedled her way out of a difficult subject: going public with their intentions.

All right, then. She'd asked him to challenge her. He would do it.

"As for being seen out and about with me," he said, "how about we start tomorrow with a harmless daylight meal in town? Dax won't mind."

She didn't seem comfortable with that. "How about we go in your sailplane instead?"

D.J. flinched at her refusal. Besides, the plane wasn't ready for flying. It never seemed ready.

"You've got prep hour right before school lunch, right?" he continued, pressing his case. "We could go to, say, The Hitching Post?"

No place more public than that.

Allaire shook her head and walked around the gate. "No way. The gossip crew meets there and, every time I walk in, they give me the running-mouth eye."

"Then face them, Allaire." D.J. followed her to the truck bed, where they dumped the trash. "Go in there and show them that you could care less."

She laughed like he was off his rocker.

"What's so impossible about it?" he asked. "Good God, why would you ever allow people to influence your life so negatively?"

He shut up while this next irony sank in. He, himself, had allowed Dax to influence *his* life for far too long.

He noticed just how cold it was, the air allowing him to breathe out plumes of wispy smoke. Finally, he went around to open her door.

"I'll tell you what," he said. "If I work on reconciling with Dax, you'll work on throwing down with the gossip hounds of Thunder Canyon. Deal?"

As she climbed into the cab, he could see how momentous this was to her. Allaire had always been ruled by the opinions of others.

Standing up to the public meant risking a tongue-lashing, and this was the worst weapon that could ever be used against someone with such thin skin.

Yet he didn't close the door until he got an answer.

"We'll see," she said.

D.J. held back a smile, knowing he'd at least won an inch in this latest battle for her.

"Maybe we should just lunch at the Rib Shack instead," Allaire said the next day while she and D.J. walked past an actual hitching post outside of its namesake and prepared to go inside.

As a succinct response, D.J. took her by the hand and led her onto the boardwalk, toward the building.

She sighed, squeezing his hand, knowing D.J. deserved more than a secret relationship conducted behind closed doors. And, for them to have more than that, she needed to get comfortable with the town's knowing about them.

All the same, she released his hand. Couldn't they work up to an announcement? How about a less obvious entrance? Walking *in* with D.J. would be enough at first.

His expression fell ever so slightly, but he ushered her past him and toward the door anyway.

Jeez, she was a mess. Here she was, the luckiest lady in the world to have the love of a man most women would die for. And she wanted to give in to D.J., but… There were just too many personal issues to face before she dragged him into her orbit of failure.

Don't think that way, she told herself. *Don't believe that things with D.J. won't work out before you even give them a chance.*

Still the gentleman, he opened the door for her to enter. Allaire wanted to brush her hand over his chest, to offer an apology for what her nerves were making her do, but she couldn't. Not now. Definitely later.

Inside, a pre-lunch calm lulled as a Toby Keith song crooned from the jukebox. The place had been turned into a bar and grill in the '50s, its upstairs rooms renovated into apartments, the atmosphere changed from a rumored house of ill repute to something cozier and more respectable. The locals favored The Hitching Post because of its hearty food and convivial warmth, and D.J., as sharp as he was, honed in on the most animated of the crowd right away.

There they were, the gossip crew, a group of retired women sitting at a round table in the bar section, as opposed to the restaurant area on the other side of the barnlike structure.

The crew's gazes fixed on Allaire and D.J. in turn.

"I'm so game for this," D.J. said.

Allaire caught his confident smile, and her stomach jumped. She wished they were alone, and it wasn't only because she wanted to be anywhere but in this room.

"D.J., can we just take a seat at the bar and ignore them?"

But that was hard, seeing as the ladies had started to glance pointedly at Allaire with D.J., talking amongst themselves.

See, what did I tell you? She's with the other *one now.*

That's what they were saying. Allaire was sure of it.

D.J. stood in front of her, blocking her view of the crew. "Is that what you really want to do, let them keep talking without having your say?"

Heck, no. If Allaire had any guts at all, she would show those women—and all the rest of the town—what they could gossip about. Better yet, she would stop caring about what they said.

Wasn't that possible?

Her gaze met D.J.'s, and she seemed to draw strength from his solidness, his resolute eagerness.

Yet she couldn't seem to move. *One baby step at a time,* she told herself. *Just take that first step.*

Allaire wrangled a deep breath, and he took her gesture as a yes, guiding her before him with a firm hand and keeping his palm on her back in a show of unity. His touch burned even through her thick sweater.

"Afternoon, ladies," he said as they neared the table.

The crew backed away from their huddle, lips still parted in mid-conversation. In front of them, five closed, brand-spanking-new copies of *Sense and Sensibility* lingered.

The loudest woman, Joelle Vanderhorst, beamed at D.J. Her perfectly styled silver hair spoke of a morning spent at the Clip 'n' Curl, most likely.

"D.J. Traub! Aren't you a sight for sore eyes?"

The other women tilted their heads and

agreed. It was clear that they enjoyed being approached by this man, a wealthy hometown boy who'd returned a success. All of them had been snacking from three appetizer dishes, and it reminded Allaire of hens pecking at a community feeder.

Another lady, Catherine Tarlton, twirled her turquoise necklace pendant as she spoke. "We've been meaning to get to D.J.'s Rib Shack, even though it's up *there*."

"Oh, you mean the resort." Nonplussed, D.J. batted the veiled barb right back at her. "If you're up for a place with a dress code, you should check out the whole complex. It's impressive."

Joelle cleared her throat while the other three women sat still in their velour sweat suits and Ugg boots.

"But again," D.J. added, as if he didn't know any better, "the Shack is more casual."

"I hear people raving about the food." That came from Cindy McAllister, who, admittedly, sent Allaire little smiles every so often when the others weren't looking.

She was doing it now, as a matter of fact, so, as D.J. thanked her for the compliment, Allaire returned the gesture.

Don't let them know they get to you, she thought.

"At any rate," D.J. continued, "you've got to see what Allaire did with the artwork up at the Rib Shack. She painted a Thunder Canyon mural that everyone can't help staring at."

Allaire thought she saw Joelle shoot Catherine a not-interested-but-thank-you look.

And that was the straw that broke the camel's back. Before she knew it, she was speaking to them. "It turned out great, if I do say so myself."

This time, Joelle and Catherine just smiled politely.

"You should be proud," D.J. said, grinning down at her.

Allaire's chest got awfully warm.

Then he addressed Joelle. "*Western Adventure Magazine* is coming in to photograph the resort next month, and they've asked to feature the mural."

Allaire tried not to seem surprised at this news. Was D.J. lying just so she could save face?

Cindy McAllister was the first to offer congratulations, and the other women followed. Certainly, Allaire wouldn't have said the response was enthusiastic, but…hey, wasn't *she* controlling what came out of their mouths right now?

Wasn't she in charge of what they were saying, at least for the moment?

It felt good, yet standing here and facing the crew was making her realize that she had a lot more to deal with than just wagging tongues. Gossip was only the tip of her emotional iceberg.…

D.J. held his hand up in a friendly farewell, leading her away while the going was good. "Nice seeing you all. Enjoy your books."

They all cooed at him as he and Allaire left. Busybodies.

Thinking she'd done enough for the day, she angled for the door, but D.J. blocked her, diverting her toward the bar.

"That was a good start," he said optimistically while he secured two stools.

Allaire shot him a mellow glance—but only because she knew the crew ladies were still watching to see just what was between her and D.J., if all the rumors about her spending so much time up at the Shack had less to do with a mural and more to do with a juicy story.

"Joelle Vanderhorst," she said. "Doesn't she

have anything better to do than lead a faux reading group and remark on everyone who wanders into The Hitching Post?"

As a matter of fact, as a lone, young, female stranger—obviously a tourist—came through the door and looked for a spot to sit, Allaire could hear Joelle launch into commentary.

"Well," D.J. said, "maybe she loves you in particular because you turned down her son for sophomore homecoming, if I recall correctly. He'd told the whole town he was taking you before he even asked. After that, a vendetta was born. Remember how she used to give you that glower from the basketball bleachers during every home game?"

Allaire sipped from the glass of water a bartender set down before them, then said, "She was very possessive, as if I hadn't earned the right to watch her son play for the team. I'm surprised he didn't turn out to be Norman Bates."

D.J. laughed while scanning the menu. Soon, the barkeep took their orders and went about his business.

At that point, Allaire lost a little composure. She was tired of holding it all in.

"Are you happy now?" she asked, not unkindly. "I took a baby step today. You can't say I didn't."

A muted storm seemed to pass over his dark gaze, and she knew his answer. No, he wasn't happy. To the public, they were still just friends, and D.J. wanted more.

Heck, *she* wanted more but…

In contemplation, he'd rested his glance on the portrait above the bar. A mysterious blond woman draped in diaphanous material watched over The Hitching Post with detached coolness. *The* Lily Divine, God bless her.

"D.J.?" Allaire asked.

He turned his attention back to her.

"About what you said back there," she continued. "You know. The magazine…?"

"Oh." He sat back, a goofy grin lighting his face. "Grant told me this morning that the editor contacted the resort. How's them apples?"

"So this photo op for the mural wasn't just a fib you spun to impress the crew?"

"No, Allaire. Would you buy into your own PR, please? And forget the damned crew."

In the background, Allaire could pick out their high voices, jabbering away. How could she forget them?

"Listen," he said. "They're already on to the

next subject. Do you think their small world revolves around you?"

Now *that* gave her a kick in the reality lobe. She finally started to allow herself to embrace the truth about why she hadn't wanted to come here and face the crew.

"It's not only the gossip, D.J." She dabbed a paper napkin at the water ring left from her glass. "The talk I hear in places like The Hitching Post gives voice to what I think inside my own head."

"What do you mean?"

She pressed the napkin flat against the bar. "I mean that I can't stop judging myself. How can I ignore the voice in me that says I'm a loser when they're saying it, too?"

When D.J. turned her face to him, she knew that he'd reached his limit.

"I really don't know what else to do, Allaire. If I—your best friend—" he said it with a particular wounded emphasis "—can't even convince you of what an incredible woman you are, I don't know what can."

She wished she wouldn't disappoint him so much, wished they could forget everything and get it together.

Wished that they could just *get* together.

But maybe it was too weird transitioning from friends to lovers. Maybe it was too staggeringly intimate to allow someone that much access to you.

Whatever it was, Allaire reached over and put her hand on D.J.'s, fighting her doubts and taking her second baby step of the day.

It was much easier than she'd imagined, too.

Chapter Ten

Since Allaire had made a big move yesterday by facing down the gossip squawkers, D.J. decided to make one of his own today.

He actually dialed Dax's motorcycle shop, telling himself that this was it—he was going to reconcile with his brother and make everyone's life a whole lot easier.

However, the phone only rang and rang and, right before D.J. suspected a machine might pick up, he disconnected, not knowing what he would say to a recording. Or even the man himself, for that matter.

How are those bruises I gave you?

Ah, yeah. That would be a great start.

Or how about the old chestnut: *I didn't happen to damage your spleen during our fight, did I?*

And maybe after they'd talked a bit, they could've even addressed what Dax had insinuated about D.J.'s absence spurring their dad's heart attack. Sure, Dax had apologized, confessing that he hadn't meant it, but where had that kind of comment come from?

What was bugging Dax so much that he'd felt the need to fight so dirty?

Now, hours later, as D.J. and Allaire reclined on a blanket near his rented cabin and his portable plane hangar, he still wondered.

In the aftermath of asking Allaire her opinion on the subject, pine trees stirred in the slight wind, as she lay on her back, scanning a clear sky that had brought on a welcome, warmer day. It was as if she were capturing the expanse of it for future reference.

D.J. was stretched next to her on his side, his elbow propping him up as he toyed with a ribbon he'd untied from the top of a local market's jam jar. Allaire had packed an early Saturday picnic lunch, taking care to include fried chicken for him and a nuts-and-cheese plate that they would both enjoy. Dessert had already been served: peanut butter pie topped with raspberry jam. After that, he'd promised to finally show her the plane waiting in the hangar after his engineer friend arrived. He'd been teasing her with the unveiling of it the whole time.

Allaire reached out to tug on one of D.J.'s shirt buttons. "Dax didn't mean what he said about your dad, D.J. Take him at that and don't torture yourself any longer. None of it's true. I was there for Sunday dinners. I talked at length with your pop and, while he did miss you, he wasn't a broken man."

Forget about it, huh? Easier said than done. "Sometimes I would call him from Atlanta, and we'd get along fine on the phone. Truthfully, those were the times I felt closest to him, when I was talking over a wire from thousands of miles away."

Allaire stared at the sky again. "He liked to chat about your potential in business." She laughed. "He even used to get this glint in his eyes during those conversations. I wish you could've seen it."

"Me, too. Dad had a hard time expressing

himself to me. I guess I at least take after him in that area."

D.J. glanced over to find Allaire smiling at him with so much compassion it stilled his pulse. All he'd wanted to do was grow to deserve her, and he just wished she would let him know when he finally reached that point.

When he finally passed all of her tests, as Dax had done....

D.J. cut himself off as she toyed with his button.

"Do *not* feel guilty about this, Dalton James," she said. "I'm here to tell you that Dax was only getting your goat."

"He doesn't have to try very hard."

Allaire went quiet.

For Pete's sake, this day had gone so well until now, when history had reared its ugly head. There was so much they had to get past in order to find each other again, and D.J. had no idea what to do but attempt to move beyond it all.

Yet how could he and Allaire have a relationship without taming what was bothering them...what was *between* them?

Nonetheless, he hated to see her get like this,

so he coasted the ribbon over her neck, up her jaw. She laughed softly.

"Tickles," she said.

He trailed it over her lips and she left them parted in mid-laugh, their gazes connecting.

D.J.'s heart gave a mighty thud, as if knocking at a door that he and Allaire hadn't been able to open yet. But they would, he kept telling himself. Once they got used to each other in this new way, they would have the most special night of their lives.

She turned her head and the ribbon fell to her chin. "So…are you going to kiss me or what, D.J. Traub?"

His blood shot through his limbs as if injected. He wanted to kiss her. Hell, yeah. But he also knew what he was in for once things got started: an abrupt halt that would leave him throbbing.

He put on a mock-puzzled frown. "What would the town think if they saw us smooching?"

"D.J.…."

"Just joking."

He curved his arm over her head, using his other hand to carefully drape her loose blond hair over his forearm. "Instead of worrying about the town, you just need to hear Dax give you his blessing. Would that make you feel any better?"

Something seemed to lock in place in her gaze. "Maybe. Maybe it would."

In spite of her reaction, he had a bad feeling that, even if his brother directly gave Allaire all the permission on earth, it might not be enough. D.J. could only tell her so many times that she shouldn't be so hard on herself, that she should allow herself the freedom to fail and not be devastated if she did. It was up to her to believe it now.

He tasted her lips, softly and leisurely. Peanut butter and jam.

"Mmm," she whispered, "you're delicious."

Laughing, he kissed her again, skimming the ribbon downward, over her throat, her collarbone. She lazily flung out an arm, opening up to the mild sun, her long sweater parting to expose pale skin where her crocheted top dipped.

He trailed the ribbon lower, over her flesh. Their kisses grew more heated. Long kisses, deep kisses.

All the kisses they'd been missing.

Allaire moaned, swept away, a searing line

vibrating from her chest to the middle of her legs. She felt stiff down there, stimulated. Alive.

She made another small sound, kittenish and playful, just to encourage D.J. She wanted this as much as he did, and right now, it seemed so natural and easy. It was only when she started thinking too much that the trouble started.

So she would merely *stop* thinking....

In obvious response to her mewling, D.J. slid his fingertips over the path the ribbon had taken: over her chest, between her breasts and lower. He traced a fissure over her stomach, as if further dividing her.

She teased his lips, licking his lower one.

Give me more, she thought, head swirling, common sense disappearing into a warm vortex.

He paused, as if in near reverence, then caressed his way back up to her breasts. There, he slowly unbuttoned her top, just enough to let the air breathe over more skin.

"Allaire," he said, acting as if he'd found himself with her for the first time. That wasn't true though. They'd necked like teenagers these past nights, but the fact that each contact felt new turned Allaire on to no end.

She ached for him to go further than ever, promising that she wouldn't allow herself to regret anything after they'd finally given in to their passion for each other.

But, jeez, there she went, *thinking* again. Yet while D.J. smoothed his fingertips over her breasts, as if adhering their shape and texture to every fantasy he'd created while growing up, Allaire easily forgot everything else.

"This is so good," she said breathlessly, her nipples hardening into sensitized peaks.

He locked gazes with her, a sexy dare for her to watch him enjoying her body. Meanwhile, he unhooked her front bra clasp.

She gasped when it loosened.

"You're awfully good at that," she whispered.

"Quiet."

The rhythm of his breathing increased as he peeled her bra away from her, then mapped the slight swell of a bare breast, circling her nipple with infinite pleasure.

She closed her eyes, unable to take it.

Oh, but she wanted to take it. Take it all.

She threaded her fingers through his hair, cupping the back of his head to guide him down to her. He complied, sucking her nipple into his mouth, where it was warm and wet. He laved at it while she wiggled underneath him, goading him.

Her blood seemed to bubble, building up a pressure that would need a release, somehow, some way. In the back of her mind, the good girl was there, lecturing her to be careful, to stop this from going past the point of no return. After all, Allaire had only been with one man in her life. Sex seemed so momentous. It was everything.

But…why stop? Why worry? Why—?

When D.J. turned his attention to her other breast, Allaire arched, prodded to a new level of excitement.

She adjusted her body so that she was all the way under him. She wanted to feel his own arousal, wanted to tempt herself beyond the line drawn down the center of her body—one that was splitting her apart even now.

Almost aggressively, she pulled him up so that his mouth latched to hers in a feverish kiss, their tongues tangling, their bodies sliding against each other.

She felt him, hard and ready, against her leg, so she shifted, bringing him to the center of her.

Yes, yes… There.…

He nudged against her until she parted her legs, welcoming him. She wiggled her hips in excitement, seeking more, encouraging and needing.

With a hitched breath, he surged against her, burying his mouth against her neck until she arched to him.

"D.J.," she murmured as he slid his hand down one of her legs and insinuated it under her long skirt.

He bunched the material up, around her hips, until she felt the air on her thighs. Her skin warmed from the sun and D.J.'s touch, both stimulating her, both priming her for what she hoped would come next.

What she'd wanted ever since she'd seen him again.

As they took up a rhythm, his arousal caused wet friction. The denim of his jeans whispered against her undies, roughness against softness.

Hungrily, he sought another kiss. It grew more demanding with every thrust, with every churn of her hips. She grabbed his rear, pushing against him with even more force.

Her mind went muddled, a mire of slow and fuzzy sensations that didn't link together. *This* was mindless passion, *this* was being a slave to desire.

This was what it was finally like to be lost in someone.

She ached for him to be inside her, and she slid a hand down between them, intending to push down her panties, to allow him into a place that she'd been protecting for too long.

Then he seemed to pause as he realized what she was doing in her fever.

"Hey," he said, voice raw. "Maybe this field isn't the type of place where we should be—"

"Yes it is, D.J."

She felt his fingers wrap around her wrist. Felt him heave out a breath and pant against her neck as he slowed their momentum.

Just as her mouth formed a question, he brought her hand over her head, as if removing it from causing trouble.

"As much as I want this," he said against her flesh, "and, believe me, I want this, it shouldn't happen near a road where my friend is scheduled to drive up within the hour."

She didn't care about his plane engineer friend. Didn't care about anything right now but the weight of him on her body, the dampness that signified she was finally ready, the ache.

The ache.

"Is it because this scenario isn't a part of any of your fantasies?" she asked softly, trying to calm herself. He'd been so patient for her. Surely she could give him what he wanted, too. "What did you imagine, D.J.? What did you think our first time would be like?"

He let go of her hand and coasted his fingers down her head, her throat, until they rested on a bare breast. Her nipple hardened again, newly thrilled by the contact.

"I always imagined a room filled with flowers and all of your favorite things," he whispered. "I always saw us together in a moment that would say everything about my love for you."

She evened out her breathing, stroking his hair while he caressed her breast. In spite of her efforts, it was still tough to take in oxygen.

"So a sun-dappled field wouldn't satisfy that fantasy?" she asked, suddenly realizing how odd it was that the tables had turned. He was the one who wanted to wait now?

"To you, it's sun-dappled," he said. "To me, there's not enough…"

Suddenly D.J. cursed while he got to his hands and knees above her.

Allaire reached for him, but he merely grasped her hands and held them to his pounding chest.

"Not enough privacy," he muttered, his voice garbled. "Which is funny since I was on your case to make our relationship public."

His meaning became clear when she discerned a motor roaring up the road to the cabin.

D.J. adjusted her top over her chest and her skirt over her legs, then put some space between them, yanking out his flannel shirt to cover the obvious bulge in his jeans, then busying himself by tossing food into their picnic basket. As a utility vehicle prowled into sight, stopping near D.J.'s closed plane hangar, Allaire started coming to her senses.

In more than one way.

D.J. had staved off his initial frustration and was taking this interruption in stride, as he'd done every night after they'd decided kisses were enough for now. But why was she surprised? Even if she knew D.J. was frustrated by her hang-ups, he was a gentleman, first and foremost.

And she was falling for this gentleman. There was nothing she could do to stop *that,* even if she wanted to.

God, maybe it was just because she was still buzzing, but her relationship with D.J. made her wonder if what she'd had with Dax had even been real.

She didn't mean that they'd never been in love—they'd felt strongly for each other, but in a more carefree way. She'd been so young and impressed by his charm and bad-boy aura, and being with the most popular guy in school had been expected of her. At her tender age, that had mattered above everything. But was being with Dax what she'd really wanted?

Had she ever really listened to *herself?*

Now, while she watched D.J. pulling himself together enough to stand and wink at her before walking over to their guest, her heart swelled. As he moved, color seemed to surround him, making what she felt for D.J. so vivid and all-encompassing.

Allaire turned around and buttoned her top to cover what she and D.J. had been doing. But that's where the covering would stop from here on out.

No more denials.

By now, a rugged man had alighted from the SUV to shake D.J.'s hand. The guys talked while the stranger gestured toward the plane hangar.

Was this the friend D.J. had brought over to work on his darling plane?

After they'd strolled over to her, D.J. confirmed what she suspected.

"This is Eric Nissin," he said by way of introduction.

After Allaire greeted him, she asked, "Does this mean we're ready to fly?"

"Whoa, whoa." D.J. held up his hands. "There'll be no flying yet. You're just going to get a look-see."

Eric, a leather-skinned man with brown hair tipped blond by the elements—or at least it looked that way—interrupted. "She's ready to go up, D.J. I don't know what you've been waiting for."

A world seemed to turn in D.J.'s gaze. A whole world Allaire was finding hard to comprehend these days.

"D.J.?" she asked. "Please?"

He stuck his hands on his hips, immovable. "When it's ready. Not any time before."

Allaire saw how alike she and D.J. really were. They wouldn't be flying until he deemed his plane ready, even if his buddy said it was.

Sounded familiar. Hadn't D.J. been waiting for her to be ready for too long now?

As D.J. took her hand and led her toward the hangar for the look-see—a taste of the flying they both already should've been doing—she told herself that the time had come.

No more baby steps.

After leaving D.J. to work on his plane with Eric, Allaire set about tackling a big obstacle: moving on.

She thought she'd been doing it by avoiding Dax since the divorce, yet that hadn't worked very well. She'd given the appearance of starting life anew, yet had that really happened?

No.

But now...*now,* she was ready. Ready for it all.

She'd gone to Dax's motorcycle shop first, only to find a sign saying that he'd closed up for an hour or two, and that if anyone needed him, he would be at the Thunder Canyon Resort lounge.

Why was he hanging out at a bar run by "the man"? That was strange for him, since he'd always preferred good times with local friends rather than mixing it up with the high-

and-mighties, as he liked to call anyone who didn't take to greasy gears and beer.

So, a short time later, when she entered the darkened lounge to find him, it was a jolt.

Actually, it wasn't that he didn't fit into the bar's rich Western decor, with its burled oak bar, sedate painted paneling and hair-on-hide chairs. He fit in just fine.

It was more that he was almost nuzzle-to-nuzzle with a woman.

Seriously, that shouldn't have been a big deal. Allaire assumed Dax had been dating all along, a confirmed bachelor. But he was looking pretty darn cozy with this particular lady in the firelight as they laughed with each other.

Low laughs. Intimate and private.

Allaire lingered near the entrance, not looking at her bag as she fumbled her car keys into it. She was relieved to find that seeing Dax with someone else genuinely didn't hurt her. She hadn't been lying to herself; Dax was in her past. He had been for years.

Even so, that afternoon, when D.J. had mentioned getting his brother's blessing, the notion had made sense. Telling Dax that she wanted to be with D.J., before the rest of the town found out, seemed right.

And necessary.

While Dax grasped one of his partner's hands to look at her palm, to trace what was probably the woman's love line, Allaire crept forward. Should she interrupt them?

Yes. She would get this done, once and for all.

Drawing closer, she saw that the woman's long auburn hair gleamed with red streaks in the firelight, that her petite figure was lush. Allaire recognized her: Lizbeth Stanton. People said she was boy-crazy and flighty, but whenever Allaire had seen her around town, she'd mostly gotten the impression of a girl who didn't contain her joie de vivre. Nothing shameful about that.

She'd come to stand at their table, waiting a few seconds for either Dax or his obvious paramour to acknowledge her.

Lizbeth did first, donning a friendly smile. Dax followed the direction of her interest, frowning when he saw his ex-wife hovering.

"Hi," Allaire said, noticing that the cuts and bruises from D.J.'s fists were fading on Dax's face. "I saw the note on your shop's door."

Dax chuckled. "Hope you're not picking this moment to start checking up on me."

"Not at all." Suddenly, this all seemed dumb to Allaire. Did she really need Dax's blessing since he was so clearly done with her? Why was she doing this?

Heck, she knew the answer. She was here because she wanted to know that she wasn't *the* failure in their marriage. That she was enough of a woman to try again with someone else.

Lizbeth's smile had turned curious, maybe even a bit uncomfortable. In response, Dax clasped his date's hands in his own, then turned his attention back to Allaire as he languidly rubbed his thumbs over Lizbeth's skin.

Weird. She almost had the feeling that Dax was putting on a show. *Almost.*

"This has nothing to do with checking up on you, Dax," Allaire said. "I was just wondering if you had a minute or two for a talk. Maybe even over a drink."

As Dax merely stared at Allaire, Lizbeth straightened in her chair, pulling her hands away from him while he held on. "I have to get back to the bar, anyway. Customers can't serve themselves."

"Your break just started," Dax said.

Was it Allaire's imagination, or was he grasping Lizbeth's hands a little too tightly?

Dax fixed his dark gaze on her. "What's our talk going to be about, Allaire?"

When she paused, Lizbeth said, "Really. I'll leave you two—"

Dax wasn't letting go. Even Lizbeth seemed bemused.

Then, as if to explain everything, he grinned that patented killer grin at his date. Lizbeth didn't go anywhere.

"There's nothing to talk about," he said, gaze still on the other woman, "especially if it includes what I think you want to be including."

"D.J.?" There. She'd said his name out loud. In front of Lizbeth, no less.

"Yeah, D.J." Dax shrugged. "Are you here to tell me you're with him? Did you want my okay? Hell, you've got it. I'm not about to hold you back from living your life. We were young, we made a mistake, and it's clear you've moved on with my brother."

He was sincere, convincing her that he truly wasn't bothered by the fact that she was doing her own thing in her own way. But Allaire had spent five years being married to this man and she'd learned to read him. There was something beneath his words that unsettled her, and she wondered if it had more to do with D.J., himself, than her.

Dax continued. "It's all water under the bridge. I shouldn't be the only one having a good time around here."

He squeezed Lizbeth's hand, and she fairly glowed.

"And I," she said, "couldn't be happier about having fun with you."

They stared intensely at each other, as if forgetting Allaire was there. But then Dax glanced back up at her.

"I'm serious about this." His gaze softened. "I only wish you the best, and D.J.'s obviously it."

And in the next second, they went back to their smiling and hand-holding, effectively dismissing Allaire.

She left the table, relieved by Dax's last words but disturbed all the same. It was in the way he'd said everything.

He wished her the best and D.J. was obviously it?

The phrasing sounded too much like something D.J. would've said, himself. She still wondered on a daily basis if her best friend— her *boyfriend,* she reminded herself with a stutter of her pulse—was thinking of how he matched up to Dax in every way.

Was competitive Dax smarting because D.J. had come back to town as such a success?

As Allaire exited, a bald African-American bartender stopped her.

"Miss?" He was holding a set of keys. "I think you dropped these."

Allaire chided herself for being so careless. These were D.J.'s Rib Shack keys. Good job. She'd been *that* distracted.

"Thanks."

"No problem. I was waiting until you broke up the lovefest between Lizbeth and Dax, but no dice. She's a little over break time already." The bartender shook his head. "They've been stuck together like glue lately, and here I am, taking up the slack."

Chewing on that news, Allaire thanked him for the keys again before leaving. While she moved through the lobby, she tried to analyze all the pieces.

A resolution with Dax had been much too easy. He'd been graceful about her and D.J., and she knew, deep down, that he didn't blame her for the dissolution of their marriage as much as she'd blamed herself. He'd shown no animosity about the subject at all, but there was...something else.

What?

Mired in thought, she headed toward the Rib Shack. Like an addiction, her work was calling to her. She wanted to check the mural over, to see if it'd lost any luster, to see if she could improve on it.

To see if it would help her figure everything out.

But when she got there, she instead found herself sitting in a chair as the staff bustled around her while preparing for the dinner rush.

She couldn't let go of one thought: Dax's sudden turn to monogamy seemed wrong, forced.

Did it have anything to do with D.J.'s coming back to town and taking up with Allaire?

She propped her elbow on the table, her cheek in her hand as exhaustion caught up with her. All the same, she concentrated on the mural, hoping it would connect those pieces for her.

Chapter Eleven

D.J. had worked on the plane with Eric until Allaire called while driving to her apartment. She'd visited her mural and it sounded as if the downtime had left her tired. Out of concern, he suggested that she rest at her place and he would stop by later that night after she napped.

She tried to persuade him to come over sooner, attempting to hide her yawns over the phone at the same time, but he didn't want to push it. From the sound of her, she really did need rest after the long nights they'd been pulling. And if they did end up hanging out, he wasn't going to allow her a moment of damned slumber—not after getting all revved up and left unsatisfied again today.

But that had been his fault. He could hardly believe it, but he'd been the one to put a halt on consummating their relationship. Why? He couldn't fully explain it—not enough to make sense to a man who wanted the woman he loved more than anything. Yet he had been serious about making love to her under perfect circumstances—and that didn't include getting down to real business in a place where she might end up embarrassed.

However, he wondered if there was more to it than that, if his never-ending competition with Dax was keeping him from subjecting himself to the ultimate contest.

What if Allaire did compare them...?

Before he could chide himself, he got to bed, missing the feel of her next to him, whether it was on a couch or on a picnic blanket.

The next morning, he was surprised when she called early, before breakfast, apologizing because she'd never woken up to call him again to come over. But he'd been out like a light, himself, so he told her not to worry.

"Can I come over now, though?" she asked.

Um... Hell, yeah?

While he waited for her, he whipped up a few flapjacks on the stove range, sprinkling them with cinnamon once they were plated. Then he set out blueberries in a bowl, accompanied by rich cream. He was just frying up some bacon in a skillet when she arrived, rapping on his door and coming inside without him having to answer. She knew she was always welcome.

Allaire closed the door to the modest, one-room cabin and sniffed. "Mmm—smells like home."

You could be home, here with me, he wanted to say.

Instead, he took in her blond hair flowing over the long-sleeved tie-dyed shirt that she'd paired with jeans and black boots. Sunlight streamed through his window, covering her. The morning promised another day of warmer weather gasping its last just before the real cold settled in.

She tossed her quilted bag on one of his couches, an overstuffed piece covered with Indian-style blankets. The theme was echoed in the cabin's tepee pictures and dark-wooded simplicity.

D.J. drained the bacon grease into an old

coffee can and laid the food itself on a napkin-covered plate. He noticed that Allaire seemed more chipper, if not a little distracted.

"So," she said, sitting at the table and helping herself to the pancakes, "did you ever get that plane flying?"

"We did. Actually, *Eric* did. Before sunset, we transferred her to the resort airstrip, and I towed him into the air with a smaller powered plane. I kept telling him we were jumping the gun, but he insisted."

And his newest plane, a treasure he'd started to call *Kara,* after Allaire's favorite comic book heroine, had flown just fine. After Eric had landed it, D.J. regretted not being the one who'd gotten into the cockpit before dark to take the plane up, himself.

Wasn't he supposed to be past the point of standing back? Wasn't he supposed to jump right in and fly by now?

While they ate, Allaire asked him more about their adventure, and he told her what it was like to glide above the world's surface, to be suspended and held up while hoping you would never have to come back down. He explained how "lift" gave a sailplane altitude and kept it aloft. How he'd gone soaring over the

Columbia River in British Columbia in his first rig, and how the hobby had occupied the time that hadn't been filled by running his restaurants.

"That's *your* art," she said, wiping her mouth with a napkin.

D.J. cocked an eyebrow.

"What I mean," she said, standing to clear their plates, "is that soaring is your escape. Just like my paintings and sculptures."

Bull's-eye.

"Hey, I can take care of that," he said, following her to the sink. "You sit and relax."

"Actually, I thought we might rush through the cleanup and take a walk through town, starting at the Square."

As she turned on the faucet and squirted soap into the basin, D.J. checked his hearing. He recalled how a lot of folks made it a habit to Sunday-stroll around the old part of Thunder Canyon, greeting each other and generally communing with neighbors. It was a pretty public thing for Allaire to be wanting.

She was elbow-deep in bubbles by the time he shut off the water.

"You want to…walk," he confirmed.

"Today's a beautiful day for it." She circled

the surface of a dish with a washrag. "Don't you think?"

Okay, he got it. They would be doing the "best friend" saunter. It wasn't as if Allaire intended to show off their new relationship. They would still be undercover sweethearts—nothing would've changed about what they were letting on to the public.

Even so, he agreed to the pretense. Why not?

They finished up the dishes, then drove in his pickup to Town Square.

When he parked, the sound of church bells struck the hour of ten. The air was still, carrying a comfortable trace of warmth as he helped Allaire out of the cab, then stood back a respectable distance.

When she slid her hand into his, D.J. almost reminded her that people would see.

She stood on tiptoe to whisper in his ear. "Don't seem so shocked. People might think you've never held a girl's hand before."

As she drew away from him, the moist fizzle of her words lingered around the shell of his ear. It was enough to get his libido in gear. Arousal seemed to screech down his body.

She unleashed her sweet, devilish smile, and pulled him toward the Square, where autumn oaks spread their branches toward each other, as if seeking to link. On the benches, people in church wear and Sunday casuals lingered; children tossed fallen leaves at each other while giggling and running around.

In the middle of it all, Allaire stopped, as if on stage. Then she turned to D.J., reaching up to place a long, promising kiss on his cheek.

The leaves seemed to stop in mid-fall, the sounds of laughter and conversation going silent.

It had been more than a friendly kiss, even though it seemed chaste. Allaire had made her tactful claim on D.J., right in the middle of town.

After she was done, the sounds around them resumed. A little boy threw a bunch of leaves in the air and they showered to the ground.

What had happened to change her mind?

She began walking again, guiding him along. When they passed an elderly couple on a bench, greeting them with the requisite hellos, D.J. diverted her to a side street, away from the boutiques and the walkers.

"Care to fill me in on what just occurred back there?" he asked.

"Yes. We're on a date."

D.J. gave her a sidelong look. "Come again?"

Allaire fake-punched him in the gut. "A *date*. You know what those are. The way you kiss tells me you've been on more than a few."

At her compliment, the ugly part of D.J.—the one he'd kept repressed—stirred and got ready to spring on him again.

But do I make you feel better than Dax ever did?

He shoved the intruder back into its compartment. "You're ready to announce our relationship to God and country now?"

"I believe I am." Allaire grabbed his shirt and towed him toward the busier street again. "I was even thinking of enlightening the gossip crew, but I don't think they meet on the weekends."

"Hold up," he said, resisting her until they halted altogether. "You're going to *what?*"

Allaire exhaled, as if giving in to something. Then she cast him a reluctant glance. "I was putting off telling you this, just because keeping Dax out of the conversation always seems to guarantee a better time. I was going to broach the subject. Just…later."

He'd gone on guard at the name *Dax,* mostly

because his competitive monster had popped its head out of its compartment again.

"What about him?" D.J. asked.

"See, here we go, getting all tense."

"Allaire."

She was still gripping the bottom of his shirt. "Yesterday you mentioned my getting Dax's blessing about us and…well, I thought that sounded like a good idea. So, after I left you with Eric and the plane, I decided to confront your brother. I wanted it to be over."

"Confront him?"

Allaire wrapped her hands in D.J.'s shirttails, bringing him a bit closer. "That sounds so dramatic, but it didn't turn out that way at all. I found him at the resort lounge and… Suffice to say that he really didn't care."

Something perverse in D.J. switched on. Dax hadn't reacted? Well, maybe this was only his brother's way of striking back at him for being with Allaire. The worst thing you could do to a foe was convince him you didn't care, that he meant nothing.

D.J. managed to keep the negativity at bay. "It was that simple? He gave you his blessing and that's it?"

"I'm sure we'll be dealing with the consequences for a long time, but approaching Dax about this was the first big goal for me. The second is to show the town that I don't care what they say."

She looked so fierce standing there, her eyes full of righteous fire, that D.J. cupped her face. His Allaire.

His.

Again, he tried to remember that their feelings for each other shouldn't have anything to do with other people. Again, he thought of how impossible the reality of that was.

"You're really ready?" he asked, stroking her cheeks with his thumbs.

"I am." Allaire slid her arms around his waist. "I realized Dax wasn't the problem, and neither was the gossip that might be provoked by my so-called betrayal of him. Gossip just gave voice to my self-doubts and put them on display for everyone. I couldn't handle that. But I will, D.J. I can't keep on living like this."

His chest clenched with the pride and love he felt for this woman. Yet there was also shame—shame that he couldn't face up to his own monsters as she was doing.

Allaire continued. "The criticism hurt because I suspected that I'd already given my best and it wasn't good enough. So I tried to stop the gossip. I told myself I should stay away from you so I wouldn't hurt Dax. But then I discovered that everything was just an excuse to never try again."

"Arianna probably didn't help."

"I hear her all the time." Allaire's blue eyes dimmed. "She practically raised me to believe I'd never have a successful romance, anyway. But I always told myself I'd overcome what life had in store for me. And when I didn't overcome, it killed my hope."

D.J. rested his lips against her forehead. "We're not going to fail, Allaire. I promise."

"That's a big promise to keep."

"It's a challenge I'm up for."

"Good," she said hugging him, "because even though Dax was cool and fine about our official togetherness, there was just something… I don't know. Maybe I'm overreacting."

"Tell me."

She paused. "He seemed… Well, he was with Lizbeth Stanton at the lounge and they were…cozy."

D.J. wasn't familiar with the name, but the

news of Dax cuddling up to a woman wasn't surprising.

"What's bothering you about that?" he asked.

Allaire looked up at him, her expression puzzled. "I heard Dax and Lizbeth are... close. Like, monogamous close. You don't find it strange that he's suddenly interested in a serious relationship now that you and I have started one?"

The question was overshadowed by the competitive ugliness emerging within D.J.; it licked its lips, satisfied by the possibility that Dax was trying to show off his own girlfriend, just so he could stay neck-and-neck in a race with his brother.

Was this a bid to downplay D.J.'s success with Allaire?

"D.J.?" she asked, backing away from him, frowning.

He realized that a slight smile was ghosting his mouth. The monster's smile.

Disgusted with himself, he stuffed that away, too, like dirty laundry on the floor that needed to be hidden before any company saw it.

He was bigger than what was between him and Dax.

Wasn't he?

He drew Allaire against him, wanting to celebrate everything good. Dax was fine with the situation, and Allaire was ready to tell everyone that she was with D.J., right?

So why was D.J. at his worst when he should be at his best?

He wouldn't allow this to continue. God, no.

"Let's get out of here and do something special," he said. "Let's have some fun and not worry about anything else."

She had shown today that she was ready to fly and, damn it, so was he.

Allaire's legs wouldn't hold her up—not even hours after landing.

Hence, she and D.J. were sitting in his pickup off the resort's airstrip. It was a prime location for watching the occasional plane fly in, but the real reason D.J. had parked here was because she'd threatened to toss her cookies out the window if he didn't stop driving.

"I had no idea you'd get ill," he said, leading into yet another apology.

Her head felt vised, and every time she thought of going up in D.J.'s plane, a persistent dizziness weighed on her.

"I guess I won't be doing much free flight from now on," she said.

Then she gripped the door handle. Even bringing up their soaring experience was re-creating the sense of dangling in air with nothing to hold on to.

"It's okay," he said.

"No, I'm truly sorry. This isn't like how I used to read comic books with you or watch you build model planes. You're going to have to enjoy this hobby alone."

Though he seemed disappointed that she hadn't taken to one of his favorite pursuits, he obviously understood. "All right, I won't ever talk about…let's just call it 'The Activity That Shall Not Be Named'…ever again."

"Thank you."

As the drone of a small aircraft's engine puttered over their heads, Allaire closed her eyes, not wanting to see the thing winging over them to land.

It'd been bad enough getting strapped in, towed up and then hearing D.J. laugh like a kid while he piloted the plane in circles. He was only "chasing thermals," as he'd called it. It's what had given them "lift."

It's what had made her want to puke.

She finally opened her eyes to see the small plane skimming the asphalt. Above, cumulus clouds sneaked over the sky.

When she looked back at her boyfriend, he was gazing longingly at the landing plane, his cheeks flushed.

Why had she been the one to bring him out of the sky?

And why did he have to do the same thing to you *today?* asked an inner voice that sounded way too much like Arianna's. *Why did he have to look so satisfied when you told him about Dax and Lizbeth?*

Without even requiring Arianna's help, Allaire knew the answer. Although she'd made her own peace with Dax, D.J. was far from it. Had D.J. taken contentment from knowing that maybe Dax was trying to keep up with her and D.J. by courting Lizbeth?

"Can I ask a question?" she said, leaning her cheek against the headrest. There, the world seemed to stabilize.

D.J. snagged his gaze from the taxiing plane and grinned. "Anything, as long as you don't ask me to dump the plane in a landfill again."

"That was a joke."

"Sure it was."

They both smiled at each other and, for a moment, Allaire forgot about all of it: the fighting Traub brothers, the future. She was only filled with D.J.—the dream of him loving her forever.

Then she recalled that look she'd seen on his face this morning, after she'd told him about Dax and Lizbeth.

"I'm worried, D.J."

He didn't play dumb. No, she could see that he was following her train of thought just fine.

"What if," she continued, "you and Dax hate each other for the rest of your lives?"

"What if we do?"

His question was harsh, but as he turned toward the windshield, she could tell he regretted it.

"First of all," he added, "we don't hate each other."

"Really. Because I'm pretty sure those bruises that are just now fading away weren't caused by love taps."

"Dax and I can end up coexisting, Allaire. We did it for years."

She actually drew back toward the door. "That's good enough for you? To coexist with a brother who lives in the same town? Doesn't it matter that you grew up together and shared the same pain when your parents died?"

"It should matter. But..." D.J. ran a hand through his dark hair. "Dax and I grew up never communicating, not unless you count the Morse code of our fists thumping on each other. There're some people in this world who are made to stay distant, Allaire, and me and Dax are an example."

She couldn't believe what she was hearing. "So that's that?"

"Why are we even on this subject again?"

"Because, D.J., even though Dax was good with the thought of us being together, he's still right *here*. You've positioned him—" she motioned to the chasm separating them "—just as if he's sitting and watching the planes fly by, too."

D.J.'s eyebrows drew together, and that muscle bunched in his jaw. He was containing himself, she knew. Why couldn't he just let it out?

She leaned toward him. "Until you set things to rights with your brother, we can't truly be together. You know it, too."

"Why?" The word had been a jab. "What does he have to do with us now?"

"Oh, D.J." This was draining. So draining.

But he acted like he didn't know the answer. Allaire doubted that though: D.J. just didn't want to *acknowledge* the answer.

"I saw it in you," she said softly. "Today. When I told you about Dax and Lizbeth."

She didn't have to say another word. D.J. slumped, his gaze going empty.

"That's how it's always going to be, Allaire. I can't erase how Dax and I have treated each other all these years. Not quickly, anyway."

"Then *I'm* always going to wonder—even a little bit—if Dax is the reason you fell in love with me in the first place. Don't *you* ever wonder, D.J.?"

Silence, pure and terrifying. But the notion had been in the darkness of her mind, and she'd needed to air it.

The veins on his neck stood out, and his skin reddened. His restraint was scarier than a show of rage.

"Never doubt what I feel for you," he said, voice jagged. "I loved you the second I saw you walk into my fourth-grade classroom. Maybe I had no idea what it was back then, but it got more obvious with every promotion day. I loved you when we got to middle school and

John Hollinder put gum in your hair because he wanted to get your attention—"

Allaire remembered how D.J. had lost it that day. How he'd usually been so well-mannered until he'd had an intense talk with John in the cafeteria. Allaire had never known what he said, but John had ceased to become a nuisance.

D.J. wasn't done. "I loved you in high school when we stayed up that night to watch the lunar eclipse and you vented about your crush on Rodney Meade. He already had a steady girlfriend, and you didn't want to play the spoiler. I listened all night and tried to cheer you up, even though I was dying a little with every word."

Swallowing, Allaire's eyes got misty, watery hot.

"I even loved you," D.J. said, "when Dax asked you out for the first time."

His breathing was choppy.

"So," he added, "don't ask me if Dax was the reason I fell in love with you. Don't ever ask again."

She bit down on the inside of her bottom lip to squelch her shame. The worst part of it was that she still had a point to make, even as D.J. sat there looking so hurt and isolated.

Gathering herself, she called upon the new bravery she'd found. She'd faced up to the public today, proclaimed through her affection that she was with D.J. now, and if anyone wanted to talk about it, they could. She'd beaten them today. Beaten the enemy inside herself.

So why was this one last question so hard?

Voice trembling, she asked it because she had to.

"Then, are you sure that Dax isn't the reason you carried a torch for me, even after I was married? Are you *positive?*"

Once again, she'd hit the nail on the head—and this time he was that nail.

In his shattered gaze, she could see that he'd asked himself this, too, that he hated the possibility of its being true.

Her heart seemed to splinter, the damage digging into her with injuring stabs.

Overhead, a small plane roared while taking off. The sharp growl of it seemed to split the area between them, ripping them apart.

D.J. had flown today, too, and she'd shot him down.

Without another word, he started his pick-up's engine and set the vehicle in reverse.

Backward progress, Allaire thought numbly, not knowing what she should say for the rest of the ride back.

Because she'd already said too much.

Chapter Twelve

In the silent aftermath of Allaire's calling D.J. out, he drove her back to his cabin, where her car was parked.

When she got out of the pickup without waiting for him to come around and open the door for her, as was his custom, D.J. halted her from his driver's seat.

"Wait, Allaire."

He wanted to tell her she was right about everything, that he was going to man-up and make his peace with Dax.

But it was a tall order. Maybe even an impossible one. Too many years had put a wedge between the brothers, too many harsh words and hard feelings.

And Allaire seemed to recognize that, because when he started to speak, she shook her head.

"I know you've got that monthly poker game with all the boys late tonight. Dax is going to be there."

Her meaning couldn't have been more obvious.

"I'm going to do my best," he said, knowing he couldn't guarantee any more than that.

She nodded, accepting this, but D.J. knew that what had been said between them today would take much more than one night to repair.

He felt as if he were back at square one with her. No—he was in *negative* squares, to tell the truth.

She made her way to her Jeep. "After the dinner rush at the Rib Shack tonight, I'll be going there to remove my remaining art supplies and take them home. But I'll be waiting up if you need to call me, D.J. For anything."

While he sat stock-still in his truck, she sent him a sad glance and drove away.

The sight of her leaving anguished him, and

he knew he couldn't tolerate it on a permanent basis. Couldn't tolerate what this rift with Dax was doing to all of them.

Dax, the thorn in D.J.'s side, the bane of his existence.

The only close family D.J. had left.

He recalled standing over his brother's hospital bed after Dax's near-fatal crash. So many things to say to each other, so many years spent apart. He'd prayed for his sibling to wake up so they could work things out; if he died, it'd be too late. Then D.J. had gone to get sustenance from the cafeteria and the doctor had stopped him in the lobby to tell him that Dax was out of the woods. Relieved beyond measure, D.J. had almost gone back inside his brother's room, thinking now would be the time to start mending all the holes in their relationship.

But then D.J. wondered if his presence would be more of a detriment to Dax's recovery than anything, if he would cause his brother stress or strain.

D.J. had thought up every excuse in the book, then had quietly left the hospital while saying one last prayer for Dax's continued health.

Funny. If D.J. had been a man back then,

he could've made the first move with Dax, but years of feeling like a stranger in his own family had left their mark, branding D.J. as so much of an outsider that it was nearly impossible to find his way back in.

Now, as he went into the cabin to shower before he went to the poker game that night, he knew it was time to finally put an end to *that* D.J.

And become the one he should've always been.

In a back room of The Hitching Post, D.J. and Mitchell Cates played a silent round of darts while waiting for the rest of the gang to settle down for a game of Texas hold 'em. This month, the only time the busy crowd could all meet was later on a Sunday, but that was fine with D.J. The Rib Shack had already closed for the night, and that was one less thing for him to be concerned about.

Unless you counted Allaire, who said she would be cleaning her art supplies out of the restaurant. That left him feeling bereft, as if she were removing *herself* in a way.

Twangy music blared from the main bar and restaurant, setting D.J. on edge. But it wasn't so much the loud songs as the knowledge that Dax had just come to sit behind D.J. and Mitchell at the poker table, sifting through his chips and brooding as usual. At about the same time, Russ and Grant brought in a tray of draft beers, laughing about some joke as they waited for Marshall Cates to round out the group with his arrival.

Their outgoing buddy indeed strolled into the room moments later, immediately launching into a story about a tourist who'd been dining with her fiancé in a swanky restaurant over on the new side of town. Supposedly, she'd swallowed a diamond engagement ring while drinking her champagne.

"I heard her fiancé did that old trick where he slipped the ring into the bubbly so she'd find it. But that's not the kicker. I heard she's faring just fine, but when they took X-rays, they found something else along with the ring."

Marshall paused for dramatic effect.

"Okay, I'll bite," Grant said. "What else did she swallow?"

Marshall tossed his coat onto a standing rack, where it snagged a hook. He'd always been a good shot. "A key. What business did she have also swallowing a key recently?"

Russ, his dirty-blond hair ruffled from the recent removal of his hat, brought his friend a beer. "Thanks, Dr. Cates, but I hear this ring-and-key story's a bunch of bull."

"And who'd make up something like that and spread it around?" Marshall asked.

Grant chuckled. "An honest to goodness modern 'urban legend.' I suppose Thunder Canyon's hit the big time."

D.J. went to the board to pluck out his darts. All the small talk was floating over his head because the only thing he could concentrate on was Dax sitting at that table, far removed from the crowd even though he was in the midst of it.

His brother had changed so damned much. Years ago, he would've been in the thick of the conversation, jesting and having a great old time. But now? Not so much.

Sympathy at a high, D.J. decided it was time to go to Dax. No more excuses.

After waiting for Mitchell to finish throwing his darts, D.J. took his last shots. Then, hardly caring how he'd scored, he jerked his chin toward his friendly competitor and gestured toward Dax. A man of few words, Mitchell merely nodded, going to the board to retrieve his darts.

While D.J. wandered to the poker table, everyone carried on around him, as if failing to notice this huge moment. Russ and Grant continued chatting about urban legends. Marshall ambled over to Mitchell, then thumped his younger brother on the back in greeting.

And D.J. sat one empty seat away from Dax.

The difference in how Marshall and Mitchell related weighed on D.J., but he was going to change that.

"My first adult poker game with the gang," D.J. said casually. "I hope you boys don't clean me out."

All right, it wasn't an apology. It wasn't even a great opener. But, as Allaire would say, it was the first step.

Dax slid a chip between his fingers, winding the small disk between each digit. Then he glanced up at his younger brother.

That one subtle look felt like a slug to the jaw. And it wasn't so much the blankness of Dax's gaze as much as the fading wounds on his face. D.J. had given those to him. In fact, that'd been the last time they'd talked.

Of course Dax isn't going to smile at you in greeting and act like nothing happened, D.J. told himself.

"Dax, I—"

His brother dropped the chip to the table. It sounded like thunder.

"Listen," Dax said, "I know Allaire probably told you about how I wish the both of you the best. And I do. There's no need for conversation beyond that."

D.J. tensed. "I think there is."

God help him, that was the truth. The longer D.J. sat here with the man who should've been as close to him as Marshall was to Mitchell, the more D.J. realized how much he wanted to start anew. It wasn't just about winning Allaire over, either. No, sitting here with the closest friends he'd ever had in his life, in his hometown where everything was so much more vivid and cutting than in his memories, D.J. saw that he *could* make things right.

Why couldn't he have a brother? A real brother? It wasn't too late for that.

The conversation around them had stopped, and D.J. knew that his good friends were tuned in, well aware now that something noteworthy was happening.

D.J. leaned forward, determined to finally stand up for what he wanted. What Mom and

Dad would've wanted, had they known what the future would entail.

"Let's not allow this to continue," D.J. said. "It makes no sense anymore, not when we've supposedly outgrown the past."

"Have we?" Dax narrowed his gaze. "Seems to me that all you want to do is bring up the past, D.J. I just want to let it go, but you're making that real hard."

D.J.'s blood began to simmer, but he fought to calm himself. They couldn't fight again. There was too much to lose.

"Dax—"

"No, D.J., drop it. I only want to sit here and play a game of poker. Neat, simple and uncomplicated. Then I'd like to leave with my pockets fuller and my smile wider. My girlfriend would even appreciate your help in that."

D.J. heard the gang stir. Had it been because of the "girlfriend" reference? Did anyone even know about Dax and Lizbeth?

Or had it been because Dax had shot that word—*girlfriend*—straight at D.J. as if it was a dart and he was the board?

Heartbeat spiking, he fisted his hands under the table, where no one would witness his white knuckles. "See, Dax, for the first time in years, you just offered me a bit of personal information. A girlfriend. Now, if you don't want to rehash the past, we can talk about the present."

Dax merely stared, as if he'd expected D.J. to react more strongly to the news that he was seriously dating someone enough to call her a "girlfriend."

In spite of himself, D.J. felt that notch of competitive one-upmanship clicking forward to another level. This was how he and Dax had always communicated, in escalating steps of tension, so it shouldn't have been a surprise when he heard himself offering a comment that would've been better left unsaid.

"A serious girlfriend," D.J. repeated. "The big bachelor finally falls to a woman's charms."

He'd meant to be conversational but, God, it'd come out awkward, as if he were setting up to ask Dax if he were using Lizbeth to get back at D.J. and Allaire. And D.J. probably *was* setting up for it.

Finesse the comment, D.J. Do it now.

He started, but his brother was already pushing away from the table as if to leave.

Russ was on him in a flash. "Hey, now. Tell

me you don't intend to march out that door and rob me of the opportunity to fleece you tonight."

D.J. realized that someone had planted their hands on *his* shoulders, keeping him in his own seat. Glancing up, he found that Marshall was the one holding him steady. The older guy sent him a slight nod, as if to say, "We'll handle this among friends."

Grant took charge. "Hey, no more walking out on each other. And no more excuses about getting attacked by wood chippers when we know good and well that you two had a tussle."

"It wasn't even a very good cover story in the first place," Russ added.

Dax shrugged off Russ's restraining hands as D.J. decided enough was enough.

"Come on, Dax," he said. "We're all that's left of our family. Isn't that enough of a reason to talk?"

Something flashed over his brother's eyes.

Longing?

Or was that too much to hope for?

As D.J. waited to see, the ringing of a cell phone hit the air.

Crap, it was his.

The ringing kept pounding the atmosphere

with its slight trill, sounding from its home in his flannel shirt pocket.

He wasn't about to answer it. Not when he was finally getting somewhere with Dax. But each trill got a little more annoying, a little more insistent.

Still, D.J. didn't get it. Hell, no.

Then an exasperated Mitchell reached into D.J.'s shirt pocket to put an end to the distraction.

"Hello?" he said, wandering away from the table.

No one else talked, everyone just measured the room's temperature with their gazes.

"Wait, wait," Mitchell was saying while he came back to the table and tapped D.J.'s arm with the back of his hand. "Talk slower. Calm down."

D.J.'s chest tightened as he looked at Mitchell, whose dark eyes held a shade of concern.

"I think you need to take this," his friend mouthed.

He handed the phone off to D.J., who stood and made his way across the room for some temporary privacy.

Allaire's sobs immediately sent him into a strangled panic. She never cried. But he couldn't understand what she was saying because her words were strung together in utter misery.

"Hey, hey, slow down, sweetheart, please," D.J. said, realizing his friends—and Dax—could hear everything he was saying. But it didn't matter, not with her crying. "Tell me slowly, Allaire. Are you okay?"

"I'm fine, perfectly…healthy, D.J., but… it's water," she managed. "The Rib Shack and my…"

She choked off.

D.J.'s veins gnarled at the hint of something gone wrong at one of his prized restaurants. But when Allaire got herself together enough to finish her sentence, his heart nearly stopped completely.

"And my mural," she said, breaking into another round of tears. "It's destroyed."

As D.J. kicked around the sopping floor and inspected the decimated wall, Allaire sat in a chair across the room, all her tears spent.

A water pipe had burst, leaving a portion of the Rib Shack damaged. But since the restaurant had been closed after Sunday dinner hours, no customers had been affected.

That was just about the only plus though.

Both her and D.J.'s dreams had been ruined tonight.

She blankly fixated on the torn, drenched wood of the mural wall, seeing her European trip savaged, seeing all the heart she'd put into making it come to painted life broken. It'd been her best work, but the devastation went beyond that. Far, far beyond.

Allaire averted her gaze, unable to look any longer. To most people, this would be no big thing, but she'd always been so sensitive, so affected by the song of a morning bird or the roll of grass in a breeze. She felt too keenly at the simplest of sights, and to have something she'd invested her very soul in die like this…

Oh, God. Aside from seeing a part of *her* wrecked, this was a bad omen. She knew it in her very bones.

D.J. cursed, hands on hips, as he kicked at a fallen plank. "I suppose this is what you get for rushing a restaurant's opening."

Then he turned to find her sitting in silence.

"Allaire." He came to her, his expression as beaten as she felt. "I'm sorry. So sorry about this. About…everything."

She swallowed, then tried hard to talk

around the lump in her throat. "You deserved my best, and now it's gone."

He got down to his knees, holding her hand and brushing some tear-stiff strands of hair from her eyes. "It's not gone, Allaire. Not at all."

She thought about the argument they'd had today, thought about everything still standing between her and D.J. Now, after losing something so symbolically valuable to them both, she felt as if those obstacles would always be there, that there was nothing they would ever be able to do to overcome them.

How much sense did that make? That something like a mural's destruction could make all those worries seem real. But the damage was portentous. Ominous.

And, really, had she needed a sign like this when the sadness on D.J.'s face this afternoon had been just as terrible?

Her gaze swept what was left of the mural. Maybe that water pipe had been faulty all along. Maybe its construction had doomed it to self-destruct.

Just like love itself.

As D.J. kept stroking her hair, Allaire tried to not give in to his touch, tried to not forget about reality, because she always did when he was around. God, this time, she had to prepare herself for the worst, as she should've been doing all along.

"That mural," she continued, "showed that I'm better than what I've been giving myself credit for all these years. At least, that's what I thought." Her laugh was dry. She was done crying. "Life has a way of putting a person back in her place, doesn't it?"

"Stop right there." D.J. had framed her chin with his thumb and forefinger, and he used them to guide her attention to him. "I can't believe it."

"What?"

"That just as I'm beginning to fight for what I want, you're backing down."

"I'm not…backing down."

Or was she?

He laughed raggedly, gesturing toward the faded bruise around his eye. "Maybe you have to look at life's punches in a different way. Maybe punches are really wake-up calls."

She shot him a look of absolute disbelief.

D.J. shook his head. "Hell, I'm pissed about this water situation, don't get me wrong. But it's not the end of the world, Allaire. What's far worse is the notion of ever losing the woman I love."

"But—"

"But nothing." His gaze intensified. "Allaire, you *are* that mural. I've got the real work of art right here."

His words hit home, right at the center of her chest. She actually held a hand there because it stung. It warmed. It tore her apart while threatening to pull her back together, too.

"You're so optimistic," she said.

"You used to be, also. And if you'd seen what I saw in Dax tonight, you might have cause for some hope, too."

At his expression, that missing optimism popped within her. Its aftermath echoed. Maybe it wasn't quite gone.

Maybe.

D.J. leaned forward and talked against her temple, his lips branding her with every word. "Dax and I are going to come around one of these days. I know things won't change overnight with him, and it might even take months or years to undo all the hard feelings we got wrapped up in, but he wants a reconciliation, Allaire. Deep down, I know he does."

This was D.J. talking? The man who'd shown such bitterness about his brother?

She didn't see how he could be so positive about everything, not when the restaurant was in shambles around them.

"Twice the strength," he said, tightening his hold on her, as if sensing that she couldn't quite bring herself to believe anything he was saying. "That's what we have if we're together. Look at what we've overcome so far since I got back to town. Could we have done all that alone?"

Her answer came out on a tremble. "Doubtful. But—"

"But nothing."

Now he sounded… What? He wasn't angry, though he seemed like it. He was more determined. Unbeatable.

He stood, and Allaire suddenly felt electric in his strong presence. Her boyfriend had grown into more than she could ever hope for, hadn't he?

"Here," he said, reaching out to help her out of the chair. "I'm taking you home."

Before she could protest, he lifted her into the air, then allowed her to slide down the length of his body. Allaire held back a low moan, pressing her face against him, breathing in his spices, his musk, and holding him in. She didn't want him to escape her, but she kept thinking that he would, somehow, someday, no matter what she did to put off the inevitable.

Love rots, Arianna would say, *just like that mural will.*

After he'd secured her in his pickup, D.J. drove to her apartment without her even having to ask.

As usual, she didn't have to.

After D.J. had tucked a distraught Allaire into bed, he shut her door and wandered into her main room. She'd styled it as a makeshift art studio, with paint-splattered canvas covering the walls and easels propped up in every corner. Clay sculptures and half-finished collages made him think of a garden of chaotic colors.

But then he came to the kitchen, which was the picture of organized comfort, with its funky rooster clock and Betty Boop cookie jar.

Allaire. Who could ever get a handle on her? Her talk of bad omens and negativity should have gotten to him. Truthfully, the old D.J.—

the one who had confidence only in business and not in anything personal—would've taken it all to heart and slunk back into the wings by now.

But he was done with that.

So what was he going to do? He wasn't going to lose her, so what would prove his love in a language Allaire would understand?

He leaned against a counter, facing a refrigerator covered with magnets; obviously her students had done some kind of project and given their favorites to her. The magnets, in turn, held up pictures that had probably been torn out of travel magazines. Most of them were of Paris landmarks: Notre Dame, the Bastille, the like. Elegant architecture whispering about the kind of history that made Allaire feel right at home.

Excitement stirred as he took down those pictures, one by one.

He'd gotten an idea, all right, one he would invest his entire soul in. After all, once upon a time, he'd put his money, his ego, and his time—every bit of it—on the line for business. He was going to be just as cocky while pursing the most important part of his life.

Dalton James Traub, the shy boy. The kid

next door. The studious one. He was going to make the grandest of grand gestures to Allaire so she would understand, once and for all, that he meant more than business when it came to her.

Finding a pen and paper—as well as Tori Jones's phone number—D.J. madly scribbled down his war plan.

Chapter Thirteen

Two days later, Allaire awoke and got ready for school, just as she always did.

While she dressed, D.J. called to say an early hello. He missed her, he said. She told him that she missed him, too. He'd been so busy with repairing the Rib Shack yesterday that he hadn't been able to get away to see Allaire, but he said everything would turn out fine.

He'd asked her to believe in that.

She wanted to. Still, even though his voice had been enough to make her close her eyes and imagine she was with him, doubt still nipped at her.

Bad omen, she kept thinking. *Don't be surprised when you and D.J. fall apart.*

So she'd gone to school, teaching class after class, eyeing her phone because she wanted to talk to him again, to get in as much time with him as she could before it all ended.

At the same moment, she wanted to put those doubts six feet under, so she kept giving herself pep talks, telling herself that she was wrong and that she wouldn't fail.

But *then* she would try to settle down and work on her Paris painting, only to find that she was too wary after what had happened with the mural. Its devastation had convinced her that committing herself to another work was fruitless.

Totally pathetic. Why couldn't she pull herself out of this funk? She'd done it before.

So what was holding her back from rebounding now?

By the end of the day, she'd told herself that tomorrow, *tomorrow* she would resume work on the Paris nightscape. That it would be more beautiful than ever. All she had to do was believe.

Then, minutes after the final release bell, Tori showed up at Allaire's classroom door.

"Ready?" her friend asked, her pixie hair wisping away from her smiling face.

For a moment, Allaire drew a blank. Ready for what?

Tori snapped her fingers, bringing her friend back to the moment. "We talked yesterday at lunch about going to the resort? Remember—the tea reception put on by the Foundation for Montana Studies?"

"Oh." Yeah, sounded familiar. "I don't know, Tori. Maybe you should just…"

Her friend looked crestfallen. "But it's *tea*. Tea is amazing. And we'll only do a flyby, unless you want to stay longer. But I really love those tiny cucumber sandwiches with the crusts cut off, and scones, and jam and clotted cream—"

Good heavens, Tori really wanted to go, and Allaire was getting more drawn in by her enthusiasm by the moment. Who needed a funk when she could have Earl Grey?

Besides, D.J. would be working away at the closed-until-repaired Rib Shack, and she could drop by to say hi and then let him finish business.

At the mere thought, her stomach went silly. God, she missed him.

"Okay," Allaire said. "Just give me a sec."

Right before she turned to her desk to gather her work, Tori gave a tiny hop of excitement. Yeah, tea might be fun. Allaire would make it fun and then carry on from that point.

They drove in separate cars up Thunder Mountain, the resort coming to loom in the distance. It spread itself over the incline like an exclusive village, wood smoke puffing out of the main lodge's chimney now that the cold had finally returned for what promised to be the duration.

After parking, Tori seemed to know exactly where this reception was being held, because she linked arms with Allaire and led her away from the lodge and up a back path, where the cottages nestled.

"The Foundation must've spent a pretty penny for this," Allaire said as they approached one cabin that resembled a miniature Swiss chalet.

"You don't even know," Tori answered.

She sprinted up the small staircase, then knocked on the door, grinning at Allaire, then opening the entrance.

After stepping inside, the first thing Allaire became aware of were flames snapping in a stone fireplace on the lower floor of the bi-leveled room. Then the rest hit her like a flood, nearly bowling her over.

The place was a reflection of every dream she'd clung to: near the fireplace, she found a miniature Eiffel Tower with white fairy lights strung through it. Another model, this of the Arc de Triomphe, was similarly decked out. Flowers had been placed carefully around the splendid Louis XIV furniture, including carved tables, a silk dressing screen and an armoire. There was even a small fountain reminiscent of Tuileries Garden splashing merrily away near a love seat.

Her gaze strayed to the room's second level, which rose above the first by four steps. There, a canopied bed boasted flower petals strewn over its baroque cover.

The air was redolent with the aroma of freshly baked baguettes, rich creams and the hint of those flowers. Even "La Vie en Rose" warbled out of a well-hidden sound system.

Swept away, Allaire wandered farther inside. "Tori, what's going on?"

That's when D.J. stepped into the room from a door near the fountain. Color high in his cheeks, he was dressed in a tux, his brown eyes gleaming, his hair as tousled as always.

Allaire grabbed the nearest thing that could keep her standing. The back of an ornate chair.

Look at him, she thought, affection welling in her chest. *My D.J.*

"Welcome to the rest of your life," he said, almost shyly. But she also sensed the confidence he'd gained over the years, and her body responded to that with a primal tug.

"D.J.?" she asked, hardly believing what he'd done.

He smoothed back his hair, even though it didn't do any good. "Sorry about the subterfuge. I asked Tori to bring you here for a surprise, then spent yesterday arranging what I could while I dealt with the Rib Shack repairs, too."

Allaire just kept shaking her head, too stunned, too moved to articulate a sentence.

Behind her, she heard Tori swinging the door shut. "Hey, luckiest girl in the world?"

Allaire turned to find her friend peering through the crack in the door.

Tori grinned. "I've got your lesson plans for tomorrow written and I, myself, will be setting up your classroom when I get there. All you've got to do is call in for a sub and manage to have a great time."

And, before Allaire could thank her, Tori was out, shutting the door with a crisp click.

Leaving Allaire alone with a man who was way too good for words.

"I can't believe this," she said, tracing her hand over a painting of Versailles Palace that was propped on a table and against the wall. "How…?"

"This particular cottage came with the furniture, and I hired the resort's concierge to find me the rest."

"D.J., thank you. This is…"

Again, words escaped her.

He walked closer, his voice lowering. "I'm going to do anything I can to show you that we belong together, even if it means dragging half of Europe here." He stopped, mere feet from her, enough to make her dizzy with his presence. "Most of your dreams are reflected in this room, and I'm here to make every one of them—and more—come true. If you'll have me, Allaire."

The beauty, the glow of the room suffused her, crisping all her doubts with the persistence of a nurtured flame. Yet some darkness still remained. How could it not when she'd spent so much time giving it a place to flourish?

"I want you, D.J., more than anything. You know that, but—"

He closed the distance between them, then caressed her cheek. Again, she went speechless, her skin tingling and warming layer by layer.

There were no "buts" now. All she had to do was open herself to the strength he inspired, the ability to think that she could triumph over anything that threatened to keep her down.

He'd said it yesterday: hadn't they come so far already?

Couldn't they go even further?

A shuffling sound from the room D.J. had stepped out of captured Allaire's focus. A white-suited man who appeared to be a chef appeared and bowed his head to D.J.

"It is ready, Mr. Traub."

"Thank you, Chef. I'll take care of serving everything, myself."

As the man wished them a "bon appetit," Allaire held back yet another beat of shock. She recognized this guy. He was a celebrated French master who graced the cover of many a cookbook.

She heard a back door close and stared wide-eyed at D.J.

"Chef Bedeau. I know him because he's a rib fan, and when I told him I wanted you to have the best meal of your life—a vegetarian meal—he agreed to do me this favor."

"You flew him in?"

"Of course. I would fly *you* to the moon if I could. You know I would do anything."

She knew. She'd always known. But seeing such striking evidence of it was almost too much.

A surge of emotion broke her down, taking the strength out of her legs as she held on to D.J.'s jacket and sank to the ground. She held back tears of gratitude, of hoping she could do the same for him.

But couldn't she? With only a few words she could choose to walk with him on a path she'd always thought to be a dead end. She could choose to embrace a love she couldn't deny anymore, no matter what stood in her way.

"Allaire," D.J. said, soothing her, stroking back her hair, "I want you to be with me for the rest of our lives. Maybe we won't have gourmet meals and fancy honeymoon suites every night—"

"Honeymoon suite," she whispered, her eyes brimming with tears now.

"Right." D.J. took a deep breath, then fortified himself, just as he had when he'd first told her he loved her. "I want to marry you. I always have."

She could make *his* dreams come true. Was there anything more important than that? Was there anything as worthwhile as facing the danger of loving?

It was at that moment she committed, knowing this love couldn't be washed away or destroyed. Knowing this with absolute certainty now.

"I want you, too," she said. "I love you, D.J. I love you so much."

Undiluted happiness captured him: his eyes shone with it. "Yes?" he said. "That's a yes?"

"Yes." She laughed, letting her tears loose at the same time. "I should've known this was right, even back in high school. No more doubts, D.J. I love you and that's all that matters."

While he held her—as if absorbing that she was finally his—Allaire allowed herself to become a part of his joy. She fused to him, soul to soul, hardly believing that she'd denied herself this sublime pleasure for so long.

No doubts, no questions. This was meant to be.

D.J. completely forgot about the food in the kitchen, where he'd set up a white-clothed table amid a flurry of flowers.

No, his world was Allaire.

Her gaze was the blue of a poet's sky, and he took flight in it, cupping her jawline in his palms and bringing his mouth to hers.

She melded to him like they were a circle whose ends had finally closed. While their kiss grew heated, searing and seeking, D.J. felt himself lift, as if out of body.

He really was the only man she would ever need.

As their kisses grew, slow and hungry, she pulled off his tux jacket, peeling away his clothes bit by bit: his tie, his shirt.

When he was bare-chested, Allaire broke their kiss to look at him, to run her hands over his skin until it prickled.

"Every time I touch you," she said, tracing his ribs with her thumbs, "I feel a little naughty. Among other emotions."

Her fingers marched upward to tap over his pecs. There, she experimentally brushed his nipples, making them hard. The sensation repeated farther below, where he stirred and awakened.

"Naughty?" he asked.

"Yeah. Almost like I've never been a good girl, or that I've forgotten how to be one. But that only makes me want you more."

She scratched down his chest, lightly abrading his belly while leaning in to nip at his neck. D.J. gripped her arms, a shock bolting through him.

Their perfect moment was finally happening…

As she worked at the button on his trousers, she whispered in his ear, hot and insistent. "It's like I've been starving myself and it's finally time to eat." She laughed. "Like I've been on a diet and now I can have whatever I want. I never realized I had so little control."

D.J. had always suspected that the good girl had a passionate side: her desires had always come out in her art. But now she had a different canvas—his body.

She painted him with kisses down his jaw, his neck, his chest, stopping to lick his nipple, to circle it with her tongue as if working him around to her *own* fantasies.

Fair enough, he thought as she got his pants open.

He bent, then slipped one of his arms behind her knees, using the other to cradle her as he whisked her off the floor.

"We've got a perfectly good bed that's been waiting for this."

He climbed the few stairs to the next level, then gently set her on her feet near the mattress, which was covered in rose petals. A shimmer of gold silk draped from the canopy, and he reached for it, using the material to stroke her shoulder.

"Oh," she said, reveling in the texture. "That's nice."

"There's more coming."

He parted her long sweater and slid it off her shoulders. It hit the carpet with a *swoosh*. As he slowly undressed the rest of her, his body became a series of bangs, all competing with each other for dominance.

Soon, she was bare to him, her skin pale in the dim light.

She seemed bashful at first, using her hair

to cover some of her chest, looking up at him through her golden lashes.

"You're…" he could barely form words "…more beautiful than I could've ever pictured."

And he'd pictured her plenty. But, before, all he'd gotten in return was a sore heart.

Now, it was a different story.

He trailed both hands from her collarbone to her breasts, brushing over the peaks of them to palm the roundness. Petite, perfectly formed. Beautiful.

Then, as her breathing quickened, he explored further, taking his sweet time, coasting down her flat stomach, feeling the muscles jump.

Stopping there, tracing light patterns, he whispered, "So perfect."

When he brushed her lower belly, her breath caught, her hand shooting out to clutch his arm.

"Shh," he soothed, heart pistoning as he lowered his hand and eased between her legs.

She moaned and leaned toward him, pressing against his body. Her breasts combed over his own naked chest and he caught fire, his erection pounding.

This was real….

He used his fingers to prime her, and she

grew slick. Then, when his thumb found her most sensitive spot, she lightly bit into his shoulder, stifling her winces.

Meanwhile, he used his mouth on her earlobe, sucking it in and swirling his tongue in time to the play of his fingers. Around and around…

Her hips took up his rhythm and, soon, he coasted a finger into her, finding her velvet-warm and tight. So very tight, and his blood jerked at that.

Their first time. It could be like the first time for both of them….

Carefully, he coaxed her back to the mattress, where she lay on the scattered petals. He spread her light hair out from under her head, and slipped a second finger into her as she gasped.

She closed her eyes and bit her lip, churning while he pushed into her. At the same time, he ran his tongue up her ribs and to a breast, sucking, bringing her even greater stimulation.

By now, Allaire was softly crying out his name and urging him on. He sensed that she was close to a climax, so he obliged her by spreading her legs and kissing his way down her inner thighs until he came to the center of her.

There, he gave her kisses of a different nature, although they were just as long and thorough as ever. He loved her until she grabbed at the petals, crushing them in her hands as she arched against him, reaching her peak.

Afterward, he rested a cheek against her thigh, sweat making the contact slick and carnal. Then, stroking his palm up to her belly, he waited, patient and undemanding.

For now.

As he caressed her soft skin, the cadence of her panting evened out.

"D.J.," she said, as if impressed.

They both laughed at what went unsaid. Her best friend was good at more than just listening and being loyal.

"I'm so ready," she whispered.

Enflamed, he stood to withdraw the packet he'd stuffed in one of his pockets and then shucked off his trousers.

Allaire watched him, perspiration sheening her skin in the low light, petals surrounding her. "So you're a boxers man. I always guessed you might be more into tighty-whities."

"You wondered?"

"Well." That slightly devilish smile lit over her mouth. "The occasional thought did cross my mind, especially when girls used to all of a sudden want to be my friend just to get to know *you* better. A couple of them would ask me for details."

"Details you didn't know."

"Only because I had no clue what was really going on inside that head of yours."

D.J. caught her running a hot look over him, and he flushed. She had to see how she affected his body. His boxers didn't hide a thing.

She slid her gaze back to his face, then sat up and reached for the packet he held.

"Here," she said. "Let me."

Tremors broke over him as he handed her the condom and their fingers brushed. Yearning sizzled through his veins while she broke open the package.

"Take off those boxers, if you please," she said lightly, though her voice was husky.

He pushed down the material, stepped out of it, revealing the full extent of his desire for her.

She exhaled, lifting her gaze to his.

It was too much to have her looking at him like that, to have her ready and eager on a bed. This was it. Everything.

Gently, she took him in her palm, then stroked him with her free hand, as if memorizing what he'd hidden all these years.

He grew even harder.

"Allaire," he said, not knowing how much he could endure.

She sheathed him in the condom, reaching up to bring him down to her, body to body.

"I love you so much, D.J.," she said, as she opened for him.

For one moment, he savored this: the woman he'd always adored returning his affection.

Then he eased into her, and she winced in sighing pleasure.

They moved together, taking up a rhythm both familiar and new. Beneath them, petals rolled into crushed buds, compressed and pulped.

He watched her as he filled her up, thrusting slowly, bringing a flush to her skin as their temperatures rose and melted together.

Time seemed to hover, silver and thick and, as he locked gazes with Allaire, her eyes went hazy, too. He joined her in this fog. It swirled around them, entering every pore with wet friction, then retreating only to attack again.

It even seemed to lift them to weightlessness, whirling, spinning, faster and faster, until he was so dizzy he couldn't think.

Faster…higher, then faster…faster…up…up—

There—

He seemed to whoosh apart, his body all air and steam, settling back down to the mattress where he and Allaire held each other.

They didn't talk for what seemed like hours. They only had the strength to breathe again, to trail fingertips over flesh in comfortable acknowledgment that life would never get better than this.

It was only afterward, when both of them had recovered, that D.J. tucked her under the petal-laden covers and brought her replenishment fit for a queen. True champagne and a tray of French macaroons. Neither of them were hungry for a big meal anymore, not when there was so much to sustain them here.

He got under the covers, too, holding a treat out for her.

"Pistachio," he said, easing the airy, meringue-and-cream cookie into her mouth.

Allaire devoured it, "mmm"ing and slumping down her pillow. "Chef Bedeau?"

"Actually, special delivery from a bakery in New York."

Clearly overcome, Allaire brushed his hair

back, then kissed him. He tasted sweetness, savored it.

"So what's next?" she asked, nestling against his neck. "And I'm not just talking about tonight."

A future. They really did have a future.

D.J. drew a circle on her shoulder. "We plan a wedding, then eventually go on a honeymoon to all the places you've ever wanted to see. As far as I'm concerned, this has been a long engagement."

"I guess it has." She sketched her knuckles over his chest. "We're going to stay in Thunder Canyon?"

Though he would've gone anywhere for her, his heart had already made up its mind. A person had to fight for what they wanted, and Allaire had been the most important battle.

Yet there was more to strive for in this town.

"I'm home for good," he said.

She kissed his neck, heating him up once more.

"Yes, you are, D.J.," she said, voice going husky again. "We're both finally where we belong."

Epilogue

The next evening, they called all of their friends together at The Hitching Post.

Allaire had even made certain that the gossip crew would get wind of something going on so that at least one member would be there.

Two of them had actually shown up, perusing well-worn menus at the back of the bar. It gave Allaire even more reason to smile as she stood in front of their friends while a ballad played on the jukebox. The gang—Russ, Grant and the Cates brothers—were at one table. Tori was at another, giving Mitchell and Russ—the remaining single guys—the curious eye.

As D.J. took care of getting the jukebox shut off for the time being as well as securing drinks into the hand of every friend, Allaire noticed Dax slipping into the room and standing in a corner. He didn't seem to be walking under a black cloud today, and she wondered if it was because of the near-truce that'd happened between him and D.J. the other night.

She could hope, right?

When D.J. returned to stand by her side, his friends razzed him, asking what was so important that they all had to be here. She wrapped an arm around his waist and rested her head against his chest, a prelude to the big announcement.

A well-informed Tori started smiling like a fool before D.J. even spoke. Allaire hadn't been able to keep the information from her, especially not after how she'd helped with the engagement surprise.

"I have good news," D.J. said.

Then, both he and Allaire beamed. Big smiles that clued everyone else in.

"We're getting married!" D.J. finished, clanking mugs with the guys once they came forward to congratulate them.

"You old dog!" Russ said, giving D.J. a friendly shove. "That was quick work."

Allaire laughed as she hugged Tori.

"Not as quick as you think, Russ," she said.

Since they'd all grown up together, the men embraced Allaire, too, wishing the new couple all the best.

Then, as the jukebox struck up a lively tune, everyone chatted amongst themselves. Tori even tried to talk up the reticent Mitchell Cates. As president of Cates International, he was quite the catch, so Allaire silently wished her enthusiastic friend luck, although she knew Tori was anything but a gold digger.

In the back of the room, she saw that the partial gossip crew was already chattering away, too. She was surprised they didn't have out their cell phones by this point so they could quickly spread the news.

Scanning further, Allaire realized Dax had disappeared from his corner.

Not that she cared, but…well, she *did* care. She would always care about him in some way.

Allaire saw that D.J. had noted the absence of his brother, as well, but he smiled at her anyway.

"No doubts," he said, wrapping an arm around her.

"None at all." She reached up to kiss him.

Their friends applauded and cheered them on.

That's when they heard Dax's voice. "Congratulations, you two. Sincerely."

Both she and D.J. stopped kissing, although they kept hold of each other. Dax must've snuck up behind them, avoiding the spotlight.

The brothers shook hands, as if testing each other out.

"Thank you," D.J. said.

Allaire was shocked when Dax shrugged, then reached over to her for a hug. She gave it to him, shooting D.J. a "things are already better" look at the same time.

Once he broke away, Dax grabbed a beer from the bar, where D.J. had ordered a bunch of them. He lifted his mug in another toast, and the gang went silent.

"To my little brother," Dax said.

Allaire would've said that he was truly in a good mood, but when he continued, she realized that wasn't why he was here at The Hitching Post at all.

"It's not every day," Dax continued, "that

members of the same family can announce the same news."

Everyone merely gaped. The gossip crew was riveted.

Finally, Marshall spoke up. "The same news?"

"That's right." Dax raised his mug high. "I'm getting married, too! To Lizbeth Stanton!"

As the gang took up the congratulations again, Allaire and D.J. applauded. She wanted to be happy for him. Yet when they were done, Allaire was almost afraid to see D.J.'s response.

But when she sought it, she found him smiling at her. And it was a smile that told her she was his purpose and his light, that they could and *would* get through everything together.

She took his hand. Her soul mate. Her partner.

The best man any woman could ever want.

* * * * *

YES! Please send me **The Montana Mavericks Collection** in Larger Print. This collection begins with 3 FREE books and 2 FREE gifts (gifts valued at approx. $20.00 retail) in the first shipment, along with the other first 4 books from the collection! If I do not cancel, I will receive 8 monthly shipments until I have the entire 51-book Montana Mavericks collection. I will receive 2 or 3 FREE books in each shipment and I will pay just $4.99 US/ $5.89 CDN for each of the other four books in each shipment, plus $2.99 for shipping and handling per shipment.*If I decide to keep the entire collection, I'll have paid for only 32 books, because 19 books are FREE! I understand that accepting the 3 free books and gifts places me under no obligation to buy anything. I can always return a shipment and cancel at any time. My free books and gifts are mine to keep no matter what I decide.

263 HCN 2404   463 HCN 2404

Name _____ (PLEASE PRINT) _____

Address _____ Apt. # _____

City _____ State/Prov. _____ Zip/Postal Code _____

Signature (if under 18, a parent or guardian must sign)

Mail to the **Reader Service:**

IN U.S.A.: P.O. Box 1867, Buffalo, NY 14240-1867
IN CANADA: P.O. Box 609, Fort Erie, Ontario L2A 5X3

REQUEST YOUR FREE BOOKS!
2 FREE NOVELS PLUS 2 FREE GIFTS!

♦HARLEQUIN®

SPECIAL EDITION

Life, Love & Family

YES! Please send me 2 FREE Harlequin® Special Edition novels and my 2 FREE gifts (gifts are worth about $10). After receiving them, if I don't wish to receive any more books, I can return the shipping statement marked "cancel." If I don't cancel, I will receive 6 brand-new novels every month and be billed just $4.74 per book in the U.S. or $5.24 per book in Canada. That's a savings of at least 14% off the cover price! It's quite a bargain! Shipping and handling is just 50¢ per book in the U.S. and 75¢ per book in Canada.* I understand that accepting the 2 free books and gifts places me under no obligation to buy anything. I can always return a shipment and cancel at any time. Even if I never buy another book, the two free books and gifts are mine to keep forever.

235/335 HDN F46C

Name _____ (PLEASE PRINT)

Address _____ Apt. #

City _____ State/Prov. _____ Zip/Postal Code

Signature (if under 18, a parent or guardian must sign)

Mail to the Harlequin® Reader Service:
IN U.S.A.: P.O. Box 1867, Buffalo, NY 14240-1867
IN CANADA: P.O. Box 609, Fort Erie, Ontario L2A 5X3

Want to try two free books from another line?
Call 1-800-873-8635 or visit www.ReaderService.com.

* Terms and prices subject to change without notice. Prices do not include applicable taxes. Sales tax applicable in N.Y. Canadian residents will be charged applicable taxes. Offer not valid in Quebec. This offer is limited to one order per household. Not valid for current subscribers to Harlequin Special Edition books. All orders subject to credit approval. Credit or debit balances in a customer's account(s) may be offset by any other outstanding balance owed by or to the customer. Please allow 4 to 6 weeks for delivery. Offer available while quantities last.

Your Privacy—The Harlequin® Reader Service is committed to protecting your privacy. Our Privacy Policy is available online at www.ReaderService.com or upon request from the Harlequin Reader Service.

We make a portion of our mailing list available to reputable third parties that offer products we believe may interest you. If you prefer that we not exchange your name with third parties, or if you wish to clarify or modify your communication preferences, please visit us at www.ReaderService.com/consumerschoice or write to us at Harlequin Reader Service Preference Service, P.O. Box 9062, Buffalo, NY 14269. Include your complete name and address.

REQUEST YOUR FREE BOOKS!
2 FREE NOVELS PLUS 2 FREE GIFTS!

HARLEQUIN®

American ★ Romance®

LOVE, HOME & HAPPINESS

YES! Please send me 2 FREE Harlequin® American Romance® novels and my 2 FREE gifts (gifts are worth about $10). After receiving them, if I don't wish to receive any more books, I can return the shipping statement marked "cancel." If I don't cancel, I will receive 4 brand-new novels every month and be billed just $4.74 per book in the U.S. or $5.24 per book in Canada. That's a savings of at least 14% off the cover price! It's quite a bargain! Shipping and handling is just 50¢ per book in the U.S. and 75¢ per book in Canada.* I understand that accepting the 2 free books and gifts places me under no obligation to buy anything. I can always return a shipment and cancel at any time. Even if I never buy another book, the two free books and gifts are mine to keep forever.

154/354 HDN F4YY

Name _____ (PLEASE PRINT) _____

Address _____ Apt. # _____

City _____ State/Prov. _____ Zip/Postal Code _____

Signature (if under 18, a parent or guardian must sign)

Mail to the Harlequin® Reader Service:
IN U.S.A.: P.O. Box 1867, Buffalo, NY 14240-1867
IN CANADA: P.O. Box 609, Fort Erie, Ontario L2A 5X3

Want to try two free books from another line?
Call 1-800-873-8635 or visit www.ReaderService.com.

* Terms and prices subject to change without notice. Prices do not include applicable taxes. Sales tax applicable in N.Y. Canadian residents will be charged applicable taxes. Offer not valid in Quebec. This offer is limited to one order per household. Not valid for current subscribers to Harlequin American Romance books. All orders subject to credit approval. Credit or debit balances in a customer's account(s) may be offset by any other outstanding balance owed by or to the customer. Please allow 4 to 6 weeks for delivery. Offer available while quantities last.

Your Privacy—The Harlequin® Reader Service is committed to protecting your privacy. Our Privacy Policy is available online at www.ReaderService.com or upon request from the Harlequin Reader Service.

We make a portion of our mailing list available to reputable third parties that offer products we believe may interest you. If you prefer that we not exchange your name with third parties, or if you wish to clarify or modify your communication preferences, please visit us at www.ReaderService.com/consumerschoice or write to us at Harlequin Reader Service Preference Service, P.O. Box 9062, Buffalo, NY 14269. Include your complete name and address.

HARDIR13R